THE FORTUNES OF TEXAS

*Follow the lives and loves of a complex family
with a rich history and deep ties
in the Lone Star State*

SECRETS OF FORTUNE'S GOLD RANCH

Welcome to Fortune's Gold Ranch...where the
vistas of Emerald Ridge are as expansive as the
romantic entanglements that beckon its visitors!

Naomi Katz is used to helping beleaguered
CEOs and celebrities repair their images. But
rancher Shane Fortune, who once dropped
her for the woman who later broke his heart?
A different story! Shane's set on having Naomi
help him find the perfect stepmom for his
adorable six-year-old. But he soon can't help but
wonder if what he's been searching for is right
beside him...and whether she might just be the
woman of his dreams!

Dear Reader,

Spring is one of my favorite times of year. Nature is waking up after a long winter, and possibilities seem endless. Maybe it's the creative side of me, but I love planning out my gardens, experimenting with what will grow, casting off what didn't work last year and hoping that my new additions to my garden will flourish. Because when they do, the colors and smells and vibrancy of the flowers in bloom are glorious.

I also love the idea of starting over. I enjoy evaluating what's working and what isn't, and strategizing ways to improve a situation. I'm not always successful, and I like to say that I'm a work in progress. Aren't we all?

Naomi Katz and Shane Fortune certainly are. Frustrated by the dating scene, single dad Shane enlists Naomi's help as an image consultant to try to improve his chances of finding the right woman to marry and help raise his six-year-old son. Despite her talents, Naomi is also at a crossroads and hiding a secret she believes could destroy how others think of her.

Welcome to Emerald Ridge, Texas, a ranching resort town for the rich and famous. Get ready to celebrate Passover as Naomi tries to help the Fortunes improve their images to win back their loves. Hang out with Shane and his adorable son, who has some matchmaking plans up his sleeve in order to find his dad a new wife. Taste some delicious Passover foods and learn the traditions Naomi and her grandmother share. And, as always, admire the handsome cowboys.

So, grab some lemonade and a gardening catalog or two and dive into this second-chance romance. I hope you enjoy Naomi and Shane's story!

Jennifer Wilck

A FORTUNE
WITH BENEFITS

JENNIFER WILCK

THE FORTUNES OF TEXAS

Special thanks and acknowledgment are given to Jennifer Wilck for her contribution to The Fortunes of Texas: Secrets of Fortune's Gold Ranch miniseries.

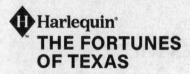

Harlequin®
THE FORTUNES OF TEXAS

Recycling programs for this product may not exist in your area.

ISBN-13: 978-1-335-99680-0

A Fortune with Benefits

Harlequin Enterprises ULC
22 Adelaide St. West, 41st Floor
Toronto, Ontario M5H 4E3, Canada
www.Harlequin.com

Printed in U.S.A.

Jennifer Wilck is an award-winning contemporary romance author for readers who are passionate about love, laughter and happily-ever-after. Known for writing both Jewish and non-Jewish romances, she features damaged heroes, sassy and independent heroines, witty banter, yummy food and hot chemistry in her books. She believes humor is the only way to get through the day and does not believe in sharing her chocolate. You can find her at www.jenniferwilck.com.

Books by Jennifer Wilck

The Fortunes of Texas: Secrets of Fortune's Gold Ranch

A Fortune with Benefits

The Fortunes of Texas: Fortune's Secret Children

Fortune's Holiday Surprise

Harlequin Special Edition

Holidays, Heart and Chutzpah

Home for the Challah Days
Matzah Ball Blues
Deadlines, Donuts & Dreidels

Visit the Author Profile page
at Harlequin.com for more titles.

Thank you to Jennifer Sumner and Katie O'Connor for help with Brady. As the mom of two girls, I didn't know what to do with a little boy. Your help was invaluable.

Chapter One

A knock at the door of Naomi Katz's sunny little office interrupted her concentration. Lunch already? She huffed. It all starts with a knock, she thought to herself as she put aside her plans for her latest image-consulting client. Whether it was getting knocked off one's high horse, getting knocked up or getting knocked out, the catalyst for change was always a knock.

Shaking her head, she pushed away from her gray pine writing desk, adjusted her taupe wool A-line skirt and grabbed her wallet to pay the delivery guy from the Emerald Ridge Café. Except, when she walked over to the French doors separating her office from the vestibule, she gasped. She dropped her wallet from suddenly numb fingers. The jingle of change and the soft plunk on the geometric silver rug brought her up short.

Shane Fortune stood on the other side of the door, hand raised and poised to knock again, gaze expectant.

Definitely not the delivery guy.

What was *he* doing here?

She took a quick glance back toward her desk. His father, Garth Fortune, was her latest client. Her latest *secret* client—he'd been sure to clarify that no one in town could know he was consulting her for services. Noticing nothing that would give that away, she opened the door.

Ordinarily, she'd be warm and welcoming to anyone entering her office. She liked most of the locals, and no one would hire a surly image consultant. But Shane? He was her nemesis.

Pasting on a small smile, she opened the door.

"Hello, Shane." She remained standing in the doorway, staring up into his blue eyes, eyes that had once sparkled across a dinner table from her.

"Hey, Naomi, you busy?" He removed his gray cowboy hat from his curly brown hair and held it against his broad chest.

Her gaze skipped from the sharp planes of his face to his long fingers and back to his eyes. She swallowed and fingered the Star of David necklace at her throat.

"I have some time," she said. "Come on in."

She led him to a seating area in front of the big bay window facing Emerald Ridge Boulevard, the main street of Emerald Ridge. A set of sheer cream curtains lent privacy to the office, while still allowing in light and the bustle from outside.

Naomi refrained from laughing as the tall man tried to make himself comfortable on the scalloped off-white settee. The delicate-looking piece was sturdier than it appeared; however, Shane still looked out of place. She sat in the matching chair across from a round coffee table in the same gray pine as her desk. When she'd designed the office, she'd gone for elegance, to match the image she'd cultivated over the years.

As long as no one asked her too many personal questions, she'd be fine.

Her insides fluttered with nerves as she wondered what questions Shane would ask her right now.

She studied him as he tried to get comfortable. He couldn't possibly need an image overhaul. His own—handsome, muscular, hardworking and friendly—was just fine. He was a Fortune, of course, so he was known for his wealth and his ranching skills. She hadn't heard any whispered mutterings from people in town. And although his family had faced a crisis or two recently, Shane's reputation, unlike his father's, hadn't suffered. If anything, she was one of the few who didn't like him.

And with good reason.

So then, why was he here?

When Shane continued to remain silent, Naomi spoke. "How can I help you?" She clenched her stomach muscles while she waited for an answer. Hopefully, he was here for something quick.

He shifted in his seat one last time, clasped his hands together with his elbows on his knees and looked up at her. "I've started dating again, and it's a disaster."

Naomi's breath hitched. This was *not* what she'd expected to hear from him. But his blue eyes were troubled, his mouth was turned down at the corners and his knuckles were white.

"How so?"

Shane's sigh was so loud and strong that the lock of brown hair across his forehead ruffled. "I've been divorced now for a year, and I'm ready for a new relationship, but no one I've dated is ready to take on a six-year-old. And those who are—" he shrugged "—don't have that spark."

This conversation was getting weirder by the second.

She crossed and uncrossed her legs. "Where are you finding the women you're dating?"

"I've tried multiple dating apps, and I've asked my siblings for help…" He scoffed. "You should have seen some of the dates they set me up on."

He held up his hands before he continued.

"There was nothing wrong with the women, per se, but I don't think my family and I are on the same page when it comes to the type of women I should date."

Shane had a type? She swallowed. "What do you mean?"

"Well, Poppy thinks I'm too serious. Rafe believes I need to have some fun. And Micah says I've had too much responsibility too soon, what with getting married and having a son so early in life."

Naomi remembered how fast he'd wed and had a child after meeting the supposed woman of his dreams. A bitter taste rose in the back of her throat.

He continued. "So I humored them, and even initiated conversations with a random woman or two I met at a bar."

Naomi couldn't help but react to that statement, and Shane laughed. "I know, it's not my style. But that's just it. Nothing I've done has helped me find a lady who I want a relationship with, and who wants a relationship with my son. None of the women I've dated can see past my name. And no matter what Poppy and the rest say, I'm not the kind of guy who dates casually. I want a relationship, *especially* now that I have a son."

Naomi's heartbeat quickened. Not a lot of men their age were as focused on having a family as Shane appeared to be. And the ones who were? Her chest tightened, and she struggled to bury her own embarrassment and separate out her issues from those of the man who sat across from her.

"Maybe you haven't given the relationships enough time."

He ran a hand through his hair. "I thought so at first,

but most of the women I've met are either only interested in the Fortune name or my family's wealth. The few who have at least appeared to get beyond those things just didn't click—either with me or with Brady."

Couldn't click with Brady? Naomi didn't know Shane's son, but whenever she'd seen the little boy around town, either with his father or one of his relatives, he'd been darling. Her heart squeezed in sympathy for Shane and Brady. She couldn't imagine anyone not falling in love with the man's son.

"I think I'm the problem," Shane continued. "There must be something wrong with me that makes me attract the wrong kind of woman. I've seen your sign outside your office, and I thought maybe you could help me."

It was a good thing she hadn't brought over her own coffee and offered Shane a drink, because if she had, she'd be wearing a latte right about now. And image consultants did *not* spill on themselves.

They also didn't sit around with their mouths hanging open.

Her head began to pound. "You want *my* help?"

Shane nodded.

"To attract women?"

"The right *kind* of woman," he said.

He had to be kidding, right? Of all the people he could have chosen to help him, he had to pick *her*? Granted, there weren't a lot of people in Emerald Ridge who did the kind of work she did. Scratch that, there weren't any. That was part of the reason why her business was so successful—no competition. But plenty of folks worked virtually. Heck, she had virtual clients. She had to tell him no.

"And in your head, that would be...?"

She felt her chest tighten. Her question wasn't a refusal.

In fact, it was anything but. However, if he gave her more information, perhaps she'd be better able to refer him to someone else.

"Someone warm and loving to my son, who wants to play catch with him, spend time with him, treat him like her own son. You know, cheer him on at soccer games. And someone who finds me attractive for myself, not for my name or my money."

In other words, someone like me.

But not her. Been there, done that, still reddened with embarrassment when the memory struck.

However, wanting to be the mother to his son? Her body heated with envy. She'd give anything to be the doting mother of a child. Even Shane's child. Just not...with Shane. Any attraction she'd once had for him had evaporated after their one disastrous date.

So that meant she needed to find someone just like herself. But *not* herself. She groaned silently.

"Shane, I'm not sure I'm the right consultant for you," she said. "But I'd be happy to refer you to a couple of colleagues I know."

He shook his head. "I can't think of anyone more qualified to help me," Shane insisted, his voice strident. "You're successful, polished, smart, and I've read the papers. I know you've had an impressive list of clients."

None of whom knew her boyfriend dumped her three months ago. She'd hidden that bit of information from everyone but her grandmother. If people knew about it, they'd wonder what was wrong with her. Andrew had been successful and a perfect-on-paper boyfriend. They'd begin to doubt her, as much as she'd doubted herself. Andrew's dumping her had rattled her confidence in herself and her own body. As much as she tried to move past it, she wasn't sure when or if she was going to get it back.

Not to mention the reason he'd broken up with her had shattered something within her. Every time she thought about it, her eyes welled, her chest ached and all she wanted to do was crawl into a hole. Even now, her throat thickened.

Thank God Shane wasn't asking about her personal life. But listening to him rattle off her qualifications made her feel like an imposter. Brushing aside her insecurities, she leaned forward.

"I'm still not sure I'm right for you." She hadn't been right for him years ago when they'd had their disastrous date. And now, he wanted her help getting a girlfriend. How in the world was she supposed to do that for him?

"Please, Naomi. I'm at my wit's end. If I can't fix what's wrong with me, how can I hope to find someone?"

Her lips twitched. If only it were Andrew sitting across from her, begging for help. Giddiness filled her. Maybe she could do this, and in the process, make herself feel better.

"Well, I suppose I could give you some image pointers, as well as a few suggestions for making your needs in a partner more clear." She nodded. "Shouldn't take more than a few hours to put something together for you. Oh, and I charge two hundred and fifty dollars an hour."

Shane shook his head.

"You object to my rates?" Maybe that was the key to getting rid of him.

"No, not at all. I'd willingly pay you double. But I want more than just a list of what I should and shouldn't do. I want you to go on a date with me."

Shane sat across from Naomi, watching her beautiful fair skin whiten. A hint of rose deepened her cheekbones and her brown eyes widened in shock.

Okay, so their one date years ago had not gone well,

but was the thought of going out with him that horrible? He tried to squash the feelings of doubt that crept along his spine.

He crossed an ankle over his knee and jiggled his foot. "Problem?" He braced for her response, reminding himself he'd have to confront parts of him he might not like in order to fix them and find a woman to spend the rest of his life with.

"I don't date clients." Her crisp voice left no room for argument.

He wasn't finished. "I don't mean *a real* date," he said. "That wasn't a pickup line. Although clearly, if you thought it was, and reacted this way, I've come to the right place. I want to understand what I'm doing wrong, and the best way to do that is for you to watch me in action."

His body heated with embarrassment at the idea. Thank God they'd never really gone beyond that one date, or he'd be mortified to have an ex-girlfriend evaluate his moves. As it was, evaluating his awkwardness with women appealed to him about as much as going to the dentist.

"So, not a real date." Her voice was measured, but somehow, he heard the relief in it she was clearly trying to hide.

And a part of him bristled. "We tried that once before, remember?"

"I do."

Now she'd masked her emotions again. Did she recall it the same way he did? Poppy, his sister, had set the two of them up seven years ago. Why she'd thought he and Naomi would get along together was beyond him, but his younger sister had been confident her friend was exactly the woman he was looking for.

Come to think of it, Poppy had a pretty horrible track record setting him up. No wonder he hadn't found anyone.

His mind drifted back to that one regrettable date they'd shared. Naomi was pretty and smart, and they'd had lots to talk about, but he was already crushing on someone else. Crushing so hard, he wanted to make her jealous.

Even now, just thinking about the idiot he'd been made him want to sink into the cowhide rug beneath his feet. What kind of a person did that to someone else? The realization he'd never apologized hit him like a punch in the gut.

"I'm sorry about how I behaved back then. It wasn't right." It was more than not right. It was *slimy*.

She nodded once, but he wasn't sure if it was an acknowledgment of him apologizing or an acceptance. She didn't look angry though.

If he were in her place, he'd be furious. He'd basically told her she wasn't good enough, that she was a placeholder until someone better came along.

Shame made his cheeks burn.

"You deserved better," he said, his voice low.

Her brown eyes, shot with flecks of gold, looked at him squarely from a face that was serene. High cheekbones, a narrow nose and a wide forehead lent an air of elegance to her, which was accentuated by her sharp, neutral clothes.

His pulse raced as she remained silent. What if she said no?

"As I mentioned, it's not really a date," he reminded her, when she didn't speak. "It's more like practice on the fly."

That got a smile out of her. "Meaning…"

"Meaning I'd pick you up from your home, take you out for drinks and dinner, and you'd observe me and tell me what I'm doing wrong."

He swallowed. That list was probably going to be long. As much as he hated the idea of this smart, beautiful woman judging him, it might be the best form of apology he could give her. He'd been an ass to her back then. Now she'd get to point out all his flaws. Of course, he'd benefit from her judgment, but she'd get satisfaction out of being the one to do it, wouldn't she?

It was the only way he was going to be able to figure out why he couldn't seem to attract the right women.

Naomi rose and paced the width of the room. She was tall and stately and moved with grace. He tracked her with his gaze as she walked back and forth. Finally, she turned to him.

"I can see how that would be helpful."

He let out a breath.

"I'll take you on as a client," she continued, "and I'll go out on the fake date with you. Purely for research purposes," she clarified.

His body loosened as the tension lessened. He nodded. "That's great. Really great. Thank you."

"You're welcome. Now, why don't you tell me more about what you're looking for in a woman, other than being a great stepmom."

He shook his head. "That's it."

"That's it?" She raised a perfectly plucked eyebrow. "What about intelligence or a sense of humor or similar interests or beliefs as you?"

"Nothing is as important as how they get along with my son."

She sat back down and leaned forward. "That's admirable, really, but also maybe it's part of the problem. Don't you want to like the person? Or even fall in love with them, or at least have the potential to someday? I mean, if the only thing you want in someone else is for them to be good with your son, technically, you could just hire a really good nanny."

A jolt of disgust raced through him. "Are you suggesting I leave the raising of my son to someone else?"

Holding up her hands, Naomi shook her head. "Of course not. But you have to realize that it takes more than liking kids to make a good relationship." She laughed. "All the women I know want to be appreciated for themselves, not just for being good with kids. I mean, I love children, and you and I would be a disaster."

He shifted in his chair. "I don't know about a disaster…"

"Seriously?" Naomi cocked her head to the side. "We're nothing alike. Even back then, when we went out that one time, we had nothing in common."

Shane flushed. While he didn't concur with that last part, there was no denying their date years ago *had* been less than stellar. His skin prickled just remembering that night. Poppy had hoped the two of them would hit it off and that he'd forget all about Lacey. He'd agreed to go to dinner with Naomi because she was cute. A super shallow reason, he knew, but he'd been pretty shallow back then. And she'd been fun to talk to—just like she was now, if he were honest with himself. He'd wanted to get to know her better, but didn't know quite how to do it. So, for some unknown reason, he'd suggested they each tell the other a secret. He hadn't expected her to agree, and of course, she'd flipped it back on him. So, he told her the first thing that popped into his head—that he wanted a family. A big family. It didn't matter that he was only twenty-five; he was ready for kids. He'd expected her to run.

What he hadn't expected was the deep sadness that crossed her lovely face.

"I can't have them," she'd said.

She'd looked like she was ready to bolt, and he'd wanted to comfort her. So he'd mentioned adoption.

And suddenly, the date turned around. Her expression brightened, they both started talking about their hopes and dreams for the future, and he'd found himself enjoying being with her. They'd even texted a little after the date, until he'd screwed it all up by ghosting her the second Lacey had become available.

He shook his head.

"Right?"

Her voice shook him out of his reverie. She'd clearly interpreted his head shaking as agreement; they were too different. Part of him wanted to argue. But what was the point? He was hiring her to improve his image, not to go out with him.

With a sigh, he cleared his throat. "Fine, other things I'm interested in for a potential relationship…"

He let his voice trail off. What *did* he want?

"It's more like what I don't want," he said.

"Okay, tell me what turns you off."

"I don't want someone who knows the Fortune name. I don't want to be sought after for my family's reputation. And most of all, I don't want someone chosen by my family."

A short laugh made him look up.

Naomi blushed. "Sorry, that was funny. Do they set you up often?"

"They certainly try."

"Unsuccessfully, I gather."

"That's being kind," he grumbled. "One of these days I'll have to tell you about some of their 'gems.'"

She smiled. "Sounds like a plan."

He watched her type on her iPad. "All right, let me see what I can work with here." She paused before continuing. "I heard about your divorce last year. Is there anything from your marriage that you can think of that you might want to change?"

"Other than everything?" He grew solemn. "We grew apart," he said. "I don't know whether we ever had much in common to begin with..." Understanding dawned. "Oh, I see your earlier point. Yeah, I want to be compatible with the woman I have a relationship with." He nodded. "But back to me and Lacey... There could be so many reasons why we didn't work—having a kid too quickly, wanting different things out of life. I do know there was a lot I could have done better."

She stiffened. "Like what?"

His throat clogged with discomfort, but he pushed through it. If he was going to change his image, he needed to tell her even the uncomfortable parts of himself so she could help him. "I should have given her more of my time. I was always either working or devoted to Brady. I think she was lonely, and I didn't see it." A thought struck him. "You know, maybe you're right about needing more than just someone who will love my son. Because she's a great mom, but I wasn't a good husband, and she ultimately fell in love with someone else."

A sympathetic smile put him more at ease.

"I should have shown more interest in what she liked," he continued. "She loves sports, and I do, too. But after a full day of work, all I wanted to do was to relax. She wanted an outlet for herself that wasn't solely about kids and pre-school and her mom friends, and I guess I just didn't understand." He shook his head again. "Maybe if I'd been more involved, she wouldn't have needed to go outside our marriage... Well, anyway, that's a long way of saying I have a lot I can improve."

"I'm so sorry," she said. "That must have been difficult."

For someone who had spent his life sure of his goals in life, Lacey's betrayal had knocked him for a loop. He'd always been chosen, whether it was for a date, a team or a school project. Maybe some of that was his Fortune name, but some of it had to be for himself, right? To be found not good enough, well, that had hurt. And it had reinforced his suspicion that he wasn't good around women. As he'd spent time thinking about what caused his marriage to fail, he realized a lot of the blame was his. And he was determined to do better this time around.

He nodded. "It was, but I spent a lot of time reflecting on what I need to change going forward. My ex and I are on friendly terms. She's a great co-parent, and we're both dedicated to Brady's happiness. That's why any woman I have a relationship with has to be willing to love my son."

Naomi smiled, and her brown eyes glowed with understanding.

"You come across as sincere," she murmured. "I think anyone you date will understand your needs and probably respect you even more for feeling that way."

He shrugged. "Yet, I've gone on multiple dates and keep striking out. I'm either out of practice or doing something wrong. Probably the latter. Which is where you come in."

"I see. Have you asked any of your single friends for advice? Maybe you just need a couple pointers, rather than an entire image overhaul."

Shane shuddered. "I can't ask my family without them volunteering to set me up. Been there, done that. I was thinking of asking my dad for advice, but…"

He'd always thought his parents had a rock-solid marriage, but after his dad came under suspicion for fathering an abandoned baby, he'd learned his parents' marriage was rockier than he ever knew.

A weird look crossed Naomi's face before she looked away.

He swallowed. His family was known in this town because of their wealth and status. He hated the hit their reputation had taken with the abandoned baby. Even Naomi had thoughts about it, evidently.

He cleared his throat. "I guess you know why I can't really ask him."

When she returned her gaze to him, the weird look disappeared, replaced by the polish and reserve this new Naomi had perfected. "Your parents have been married for a long time," she conceded. "I suspect things have changed since the last time they dated."

Maybe she didn't know about the baby. Or she didn't think it was a knock on their reputation, even though the allegations against Garth had been proven false. Or, perhaps, she didn't want to talk badly about his family. Regardless, he wasn't about to delve too deeply into her feelings about it. He needed her to help him.

"So, how soon can we have our trial date?" he asked.

Naomi looked at her tablet and swiped through to what he assumed was her calendar. "How about next week?"

So long? His stomach dropped. It had taken a lot out of him to get up the nerve to ask her to help him. He'd paced outside her office before daring to enter, and that was after an entire week of picking up the phone to call her, but changing his mind. If he waited too long, he might be tempted to forego the whole thing.

"If that's the soonest you can do, then fine. I was thinking of lunch," Shane said. "At Captain's."

She raised an eyebrow. "You want to go to the penthouse restaurant at the Emerald Ridge Hotel? With *me*?"

"If we're going to simulate a date, it should be someplace I would take a date, right? Besides, their seafood is fantastic."

For a second, she looked like she was going to protest. "You're right." She looked again at her tablet. "Actually, if it's just lunch, I'm free on Thursday at twelve thirty, but I have a meeting at two."

He smiled, relief washing over him. Putting it on the calendar would ensure she wouldn't back out. Or him. And if anyone was going to pick apart his image, he wanted it to be someone he knew. "I'll make the reservation and pick you up." He looked around. "From here, or from home?"

"From here will be fine," she replied. "I guess it's a date."

"Jean, it would be helpful if you prioritized which tasks are more critical than others," Naomi said later that afternoon via Zoom. This was her third meeting with one of her most difficult clients, and while focusing on improving the woman's management style helped keep her mind off Shane, she needed a break.

"Everything my company does is important, Naomi."

She clenched her fist out of sight of the camera. "Of course, it is. But if you act like there's always a five-alarm fire, your employees are going to ignore the smell of smoke until the flames burn the building to the ground."

A terrible metaphor, but one she hoped Jean would finally listen to. Otherwise, she'd have to be blunter. The woman's publicity firm was in crisis. Her employees hated their boss's micromanagement style, and the clients were ready to bolt. Jean had hired her as a last-ditch effort, but unless the woman started taking some of her suggestions to heart, there was no way Naomi was going to be able to help her out.

Her throat thickened. Was she somehow losing her touch? She gave herself a firm, invisible shake and reminded herself of the mantra she'd learned to recite after her breakup—she was smart, she was good, and *she was enough*. Just because Andrew had dumped her and rocked her self-confidence, didn't mean she wasn't great at her job.

"My name is on the door, Naomi. My reputation demands that our work be perfect."

"Your name is your brand. But there's a difference between associating your name with perfection or misery." Naomi sighed. "You came to me because you want to improve your brand, your image. Improvement takes change, hard change sometimes."

There was silence on the other end of the line.

Naomi rubbed her eyes and paced her office in her stockinged feet while she waited for a response.

"All right," Jean said, her tone skeptical. "I'll make the list."

She let out a sigh of relief and a silent cheer. "While you're making that list, make a second list of three to five things you want your brand to be synonymous with. We'll talk next week and go over them."

Clicking out of the Zoom meeting, Naomi threw her head back and groaned. She loved her job. She really did. But Jean was the type of client who frustrated her the most. The kind who clearly needed help but was reluctant to accept it. Who expected results but was resistant to put in the work.

Would Shane be that way?

She didn't think so. He was quick to point out his own faults. She'd asked him about his divorce and expected him to blame his ex-wife. But he hadn't. She chastised herself for jumping to conclusions and vowed to be more accepting in the future.

A timid knock on the door—one that barely registered—made Naomi swing around and glance at the clock above it. Her new client. Taking a deep breath to cleanse herself from the frustrations of the last meeting, she strode forward and opened the door.

"M-Ms. Katz?" A pale woman with light brown hair stood in the doorway, barely able to make eye contact with her.

"Yes, I'm Naomi. You must be Alfreda."

The woman nodded.

"Come on inside." Naomi swung the door wide and held her arm out to indicate the seating area by the bay window of her office, the same place she'd sat with Shane earlier. With an apologetic look, the woman scurried inside and sat at the very edge of the sofa, hands clenched in her lap.

"Would you like anything to drink?" Naomi offered.

"Um, water would be nice, if it isn't too much trouble."

She went into the kitchenette and returned carrying a tray with a pitcher of cucumber water and two glasses. She poured the drinks and then sat across from Alfreda, taking in her mannerisms and dress. The petite woman wore a light blue pantsuit that brought out the color of her eyes and emphasized her fair skin. She dressed well. The cloth was expensive, and the suit was tailored to fit her petite frame.

"How can I help you?" Naomi asked gently.

Alfreda's cheeks reddened as she spoke. "I've been working for my accounting firm for two years now. I've brought in several new clients, and I'd like to ask for a raise, but I don't know how. I've tried several times, but I chicken out at the last minute, and I was hoping you could help me."

The woman didn't need help asking for a raise, she

needed more confidence. Insecurity oozed from every pore, and sympathy filled Naomi. She knew what it was like to doubt yourself. Alfreda was a good reminder, though, not to let the insecurity she'd felt after Andrew go too far.

"Okay, Alfreda—"

"My friends call me Allie."

Naomi liked how she'd interrupted her. She had potential for improvement.

"Okay, Allie, have your bosses given you any performance reviews?"

She nodded.

"And how were they?"

"Positive."

"Great." Naomi asked a number of questions—some standard that she asked all her clients and others targeted to Allie's specific situation. It took some doing to get her timid client to give detailed answers. She leaned toward one- and two-word replies, and she kept her voice low. At times, Naomi had to strain to hear her.

"I think it's important that you do ask for a raise," Naomi said. "As women, we tend to undervalue ourselves, and asking for compensation equivalent to our worth is one of the toughest things for most of us to do. But in order to do it effectively, you have to not only ask for it, but believe you *deserve* it." Naomi leaned back and crossed her legs. "To that end, I'd like you to put together a list of your positive traits."

Allie's eyes widened. "Right now?"

"No, before our next meeting. Write out a list of everything about yourself—physical, emotional, mental, occupational—that is good. And when you come back, we're going to go over the list together."

A combination of skepticism and fear made Allie blink quickly. She clasped and unclasped her hands.

"How is that going to help me get a raise?"

"As I mentioned, in order to ask for a raise, you have to be confident that you are worthy of it. We're going to discuss all the positive traits you possess to increase your self-worth, so that when the time comes for you to ask for more money, you'll be successful."

"Okay." Allie didn't look convinced, but Naomi coordinated schedules and they made plans to meet again next week.

As her new client left her office, Naomi's phone rang.

"Naomi Katz, Image Consultant. This is Naomi."

"Naomi, Garth Fortune here. Was that my son, Shane, leaving your office earlier today?"

Naomi paused. Was he spying on her? "Yes, it was," she said, jaw tight.

The older man cleared his throat. "I hope you kept our arrangement confidential. The last thing I want is my son knowing what I'm doing."

She tried not to take offense at his words...or his tone. Men like Garth were the epitome of Texas alpha men and didn't like admitting to weaknesses. Even if what he was doing was a good thing.

"No, Garth, I'd never tell anyone about you. You have nothing to worry about."

His sigh of relief echoed through the phone. "Good." He chuckled. "I guess I still have more work to do on myself. Sorry if I jumped at you."

She smiled. "Hey, at least you're recognizing the issue after the fact. Now we just have to get you to prevent it from happening in the first place."

His laughter boomed across the phone line. "That's what I like about you, Naomi. You've got a great sense of humor."

"If it helps you to take my advice more often, it'll continue," she murmured.

"You drive a hard bargain."

"And I keep my clients confidential."

The man sobered. "Thank you. I appreciate it. I won't doubt you again."

Ending the call, Naomi grabbed her jacket and purse, locked up her office and drove her Jeep to Emerald Ridge Grocery, located on a side street off Emerald Ridge Boulevard. The high-end supermarket offered lots of gourmet takeout, a salad bar, an international section and a delicious bakery. Naomi loved the kosher products they carried. On the way, she called her grandmother.

"Hi, Bubbe, it's me. I'm stopping at the store on my way to you. What do you need?"

"You know, *bubbelah*, if you just bought a week's worth of groceries at once, it would be easier on you."

While her parents were traveling, Naomi had taken on helping her grandmother out as much as possible. Picking up groceries was an easy task and ensured she could stop by to see her Bubbe as well. She pulled into the parking lot at the back of the limestone-fronted store and engaged the parking brake. "But what if you're in the mood for fish, and I buy chicken? Or you want something sweet, and I purchase salty?"

"If you buy me something salty, my sodium levels are going to skyrocket, and the doctor is going to yell at me. And I'm going to tell her it's your fault," Bubbe said.

"Way to throw me under the bus." Naomi laughed. "But seriously, with Passover coming up, I thought we could start prepping early. I'll pick up the matzah ball soup ingredients today."

"Good idea. And don't forget the oranges for my citrus olive oil Passover cake."

Naomi swiped the phone screen to find her grocery app. "Oranges, got it. I'll be at your place in half an hour. Love you!"

"Love you more."

The warm feeling carried Naomi through the aisles of the upscale grocery store, the self-checkout lane and all the way back to her grandmother's charming garden apartment. Bubbe had lived here for most of Naomi's adult life, led an active social life and was good friends with many of her neighbors.

She traveled the winding walkway through lavender phlox blooms and yellow primroses. The cheerful colors filled her with joy as she let herself into her grandmother's apartment. She inhaled the familiar scent of lemony Pine-Sol.

"Hi, Bubbe!" she called.

Her grandmother, whose head reached Naomi's shoulder, rushed over from the bedroom and squeezed Naomi's waist. "Hello, *bubbelah*. I was just dusting the bedroom. Come into the kitchen."

Naomi followed the white-haired bundle of energy into the modern gray kitchen—the monotony alleviated with splashes of blue and green—and put the grocery bag on the black granite counter.

"Have you heard from your parents recently?" her grandmother asked.

"I got an email yesterday from Tuscany," Naomi replied. "It sounds like they're having a wonderful time."

"Good, good, good. I hope they bring me back some good olive oil."

"I'll mention it to them the next time we text," Naomi said. She pulled out a fillet of salmon and stuck it in the stainless-steel fridge. "That's for dinner tonight."

"Wonderful. I'll make it with some Old Bay and spinach." She peered into the grocery bag. "You bought more spice, right?"

Naomi held it up. "Of course, I did. I'm surprised you don't insist on putting it in the soup."

Her grandmother laughed. "Just you wait. One year, I might." The woman sighed. "Your grandfather introduced me to the flavor, you know."

Naomi put her arm around the old woman's shoulders and squeezed. Even after ten years, his absence hurt both of them. "I miss him, too."

Clearing her throat, her grandmother reached under the stove for her soup pot. "Enough sadness. Grab the chicken from the fridge, please?"

As they made the soup, Naomi told her grandmother about her day, leaving out Garth Fortune's name.

"Your business is doing well, *bubbelah*. I'm so proud of you."

"Thank you. I'm nervous about this lunch with Shane though."

"I can see why," her grandmother said. "That man is gorgeous."

"Bubbe!"

"Don't *Bubbe* me, Naomi. I'm old, not dead. And he is gorgeous."

Privately, Naomi agreed. He'd been good-looking when she'd gone out with him seven years ago, and the man only got better with age. His face had filled out a little, but still retained his high cheekbones. When he smiled, parentheses formed on either side of his mouth, and his blue eyes glimmered. And when he was serious, like he'd been in her office, they darkened to a deep blue. His shoulders were broad, and his clothes fit him well. In another life, she'd be attracted to him. But he was her client, and their one date had been a hot mess.

Her grandmother nudged her.

"Yes, he's good-looking. But his looks are irrelevant to me since he's my client. I'm focusing on his overall image—how he acts, what he says, etcetera. I'm critiquing him."

Bubbe's eyes glinted. "All the more reason to admire him, you mean."

"Ugh."

Her grandmother's laugh, which sounded more like a cackle, made her shake her head.

"Not paying attention to his looks. *Ha!* You'd have to be blind. But seriously, what are you nervous about? You're a pro at your job. Lots of good-looking men have hired you, even famous actors. Why is Shane different?"

"I don't know. I'm just…not sure I can separate personal from professional with him. I don't want to get into the same situation as I did before."

"Naomi, you went on one date with him years ago, and it didn't work out. Tell me something. Are you willing to date someone who isn't Jewish?"

Naomi bit her lip. "You and Mom and Dad have always stressed how much easier a relationship is when both people are from the same religion or culture."

Her grandmother nodded.

"And I get that. I'm just not sure I'm ready to say absolutely not. Heck, I'm not even sure I'm ready to start dating anyone again."

"Well, then, this is a business lunch. You're advising him. I don't see what the issue is."

Put like that, neither did Naomi. "I guess because he's someone I know and have a little history with. Maybe I'm more self-conscious?"

Bubbe patted her hand. "You have nothing to be worried about. You're beautiful, intelligent, poised."

"And I'm your granddaughter."

The old woman laughed. "And you're my granddaughter. You'll be wonderful. Now, let's get started on the Passover baking…"

Chapter Two

"Kevin is great, Dad," Brady said to Shane as they ate dinner that night.

His son was bright and friendly. He noticed everything, and had a funny way of looking at things. Brady never failed to entertain or impress his dad, and eating together made Shane feel closer to him.

"I'm glad you like him. I do, too."

Kevin was his ex's soon-to-be second husband. Shane respected the man, and thought he was a perfect fit for his ex-wife. And he treated Brady like his own son, which was important to Shane.

"He took me to the museum the other day. We saw all these cool dinosaurs, like a T. rex and a Stegosaurus. Did you know a Stegosaurus has these cool spiky things on their backs? Kevin said they're called kites. Isn't that funny? I thought kites were what you flew in the sky. And he said the next time it's windy out, we'll make some. Kites, not Stegosauruses."

"That sounds awesome, kiddo. You finished with your hamburger?"

"Almost," he said, his mouth full of food.

"Dude, no talking with your mouth full. No one wants to see that."

Brady giggled, opened his mouth again, then quickly listened when Shane gave him a look. He swallowed his food. "Mom and Kevin are getting married soon. When are you getting married?"

Shane choked on his last bite of burger. "I don't know, bud. Whenever I find someone I want to marry, I suppose."

Brady nodded. "I think you should find one soon. If I'm going to have a stepdad, I should have a stepmom, too."

Shane arched a brow and began clearing their plates.

The six-year-old jumped down from his chair and started helping.

"Oh really," Shane asked, loading the dishwasher. "Why?"

"More people who think I'm cool." His son gave him a huge grin.

Shane laughed. "Not sure that's the best reason to get married, Brady."

"Why not? Besides, that way I could have a mom and dad at each house."

After ruffling his son's brown hair, Shane wiped down the table and followed him into the family room. "Someday, you're going to laugh at that idea."

"I will not. Besides, Mom is super happy with Kevin, and I want you to be happy with someone, too."

"Aww, that's sweet."

Shane looked fondly at his son as they played a video game together. He'd lucked out with this one, and he was sure a woman was out there who would love him as much as he did. He just needed to find her. Sighing, he wiped his palms on his thighs, hoping Naomi would be able to help him.

Later that evening, after Shane oversaw Brady's shower and bedtime routine, he was tucking him into bed when the kid asked, "How do you get a wife, anyway?"

If I only knew. Shane took a moment to collect himself. "Well, I'd have to meet a woman who loved me as much as I loved her. Then we'd date for a little while, and I'd introduce her to you. And then if you liked her, too, we'd get married with a wedding, just like your mom is going to have."

Brady nodded, yawning.

"You need to buy her a pretty ring, Dad. Kevin bought Mom a diamond ring, and she cried when he gave it to her. I got mad at Kevin, but he told me that women cry sometimes when they're happy."

He touched his son on the shoulder, his chest expanding with pride at his boy's fierce protectiveness toward his mother. "That's right, they do." He remembered lots of times he and Lacey had cried from happiness, like when Brady was born.

"He's gonna move into our house when they're married. Your wife would have to move in here, too, but not in my room. She'd have to move in with you."

Shane nodded. "Yes, that's what happens, bud." He silently begged his son not to ask why. Luckily, the kid had already moved on to the next thing on his list.

"So you need to find someone who likes you, Dad."

"I will." His answer expressed way more confidence than he felt. Shane thought about his upcoming lunch with Naomi. Hopefully, she'd figure out what he was doing wrong so that he could start dating the right women.

"How are you going to do that?" Brady grabbed his stuffed animal and snuggled into bed. "I know, I know!" All of a sudden, his tired son got a second wind. "You should marry someone who shares snacks with you!"

Shane couldn't help himself. He burst out laughing. "Brady, who do I eat snacks with?" He poked his son in the belly. "You," he said. "I eat snacks with you. Should I marry you?"

Now it was Brady's turn to laugh, and like most young boys, that involved falling out of his bed and rolling around on the floor, giggling, until he finally got up, brushed himself off and climbed back under the covers.

"You can't marry me, Dad. I'm your son."

"Exactly."

"Hmm." Brady scrunched up his face, thinking hard.

God, this kid is adorable. No matter what woman he ended up with, it had to be someone who could love Brady as much as he did.

"I know what to do," Brady burst out. "We should go to the LEGO store!"

He reared back. This was new. "What's at the LEGO store? Other than LEGO bricks, I mean."

"Well, I like building LEGO models, and you like building them with me, so maybe we can find a girl who likes LEGO, and you can marry her."

Shane tousled his son's brown hair. "Mmm, I'm not sure I'm going to find many single women in the LEGO store, but it sure would be nice if the woman I find likes them, wouldn't it?"

Brady nodded. "We could have LEGO nights together."

"That would be super fun," Shane agreed.

He wondered what kind of image transformation he'd need to find a woman who liked LEGO bricks and laughed to himself.

"Okay, bud, time for bed." Leaning over, he kissed his son's cheek, adjusted his red plaid comforter and switched off the light. Closing the door, but leaving it open a crack, he went downstairs to the family room, turned on a baseball game and grabbed his phone to text his ex a little about their day. It wasn't necessary. She trusted him and he her. But they liked to keep each other aware of things. Plus, she'd get a kick out of the LEGO story.

Finished with the update, he watched the end of the Rangers game, pumping his fist in the air when they won. Then he locked up the house, made a last check on Brady and got ready for bed. Between the Rangers' win and the kid's funny perspective on how to pick up women, he was in a good mood. He smiled, thinking about his son. Finding a woman who could love Brady as much as he did shouldn't be hard, in theory. The kid was great. When he had lunch with Naomi, he'd find out how he could make himself more attractive to the elusive woman who would be his perfect life partner.

At least, he hoped he would. He couldn't be that much of a lost cause. Besides, her fees were high enough.

He shook his head. He didn't begrudge Naomi her fees. He'd heard how successful she was and had even learned a story or two about people she'd supposedly helped. Rumor had it, she'd helped Betina Blackfoot improve her professional image, enabling her to land a top managerial position at Fortune's Gold Guest Ranch and Spa after her kids were born and she returned to the workforce.

Naomi even worked with a few celebrities, if the local rumors were true. The woman had always been good at guiding people toward their goals. He remembered Poppy telling him a few stories about how helpful Naomi was. One he remembered happened in high school. Poppy had been trying to decide what to do with her future. The guidance counselor hadn't done anything more than hand her a bunch of brochures. Naomi had sat down with her, asked several pointed questions, and next thing he knew, his sister was headed to college for business management. Now, she ran the family's spa and was incredibly successful. Unless, of course, that story had just been Poppy trying to hype her up, so he'd date her.

He replayed images of Naomi as he lay in bed. She sure was beautiful.

She was pretty seven years ago when they'd gone on their date, but she was even more breathtaking now. She had a polish to her, not just in the way she presented herself, but her fair skin glowed, her brown eyes shone and her brunette hair had a luster, even twisted up behind her head as it had been this afternoon.

Too bad she was already dating someone. His sister had mentioned she was in a long-term relationship with some guy. *Lucky bastard.*

Although they hadn't worked out back then, he would have liked to try again with her.

Come to think of it, what kind of guy was she seeing? And how long-term was it? She lived and worked in town, yet he hadn't spotted her with anyone.

He cringed, thinking about how awkward he'd been with her. Rather than easing into getting to know her back then, he'd blurted out how much he wanted a family and asked her to confess a secret. Talk about a lack of social skills. He'd basically told her he was looking for a baby machine.

Shane ran a hand over his eyes and groaned.

He'd coasted on his family name and reputation, which afforded him popularity and obvious wealth, but the truth was, he'd always been awkward and unsure around girls. His lack of confidence continued as he grew older, even if he were better able to hide it now. For most of his life, he'd used his Fortune name as a shield. No wonder other women looked to him as a way for them to be rich society wives. Women expected him to wine and dine them, when deep inside, he'd just been looking for a way to connect. And sometimes, he flubbed, big time. Like he had with Naomi.

It was a good thing she was taken now, or he'd be tempted to ask her out and show her how he'd changed. *If* he'd changed. He shook his head. That would only make things more uncomfortable between them, especially since he needed her help. Clearly, he hadn't yet put his never-ending awkward phase behind him.

Still, sitting with her today, she'd drawn him in. Even though, admittedly, they were complete opposites. He'd never cared about his image, and that was her *career.* She was Jewish, and he wasn't. She couldn't have kids, and he wanted them. Although adoption could solve that hurdle. But the religion part? He didn't mind their differences. He wasn't particularly observant, but he didn't know if she was. He'd have to find out.

He shook his head. He didn't have to find out anything. They weren't going to date, so it was irrelevant.

The next day, after dropping Brady at school and grabbing a coffee from Coffee Connection, his favorite local café, Shane headed back to the guest ranch. He drove his truck through the ornate iron gates of the property and wound his way behind the main house. Even though he'd grown up in one wing of the huge house, the sight of it always filled him with awe. Especially since the cavernous house was now practically empty, other than his parents and aunt and uncle, who lived in separate wings. As usual, he shrugged to himself at the unusual arrangement that somehow worked and drove the half mile to the ranch office. One of the ranch hands had already checked on the fifty horses owned by the guest and cattle ranch and brought him the daily report.

Shane scanned it and nodded. "Make sure the vet checks Bluebonnet, Pecan and Houston Black. I don't want them put back into the riding rotation at the ranch unless they're completely fit."

"She's already scheduled to stop by later today," Raul said.

"Good. The feed costs are looking high. See if we can negotiate a better price, and if not, have Rafe start looking into other options."

Raul made notes.

"And we're down two hands today?"

"Yeah, it's the stomach bug that's been going around."

Shane nodded before handing the report back to Raul. "Okay. Let me know if you run into any problems, and if you need to, borrow some help from the cattle ranch."

Raul sauntered off, leaving Shane to take care of some paperwork at his desk. A knock on his door made him look up.

"Hey, Mom." He rose from his chair, kissed Shelley's cheek and pulled out one of the chairs on the other side of his desk for her to sit. "You don't usually come over to this side of the ranch." His mother was tall and stately, with a quick smile and love that shone through every glance she gave. Impeccably dressed, she made even her jeans and sweater look glamorous.

"I was talking to Aunt Darla earlier. She mentioned the thefts at the area ranches, and I'm worried."

"I am, too," he admitted. "We still haven't found our missing mare, Butter. Rafe's as concerned as I am."

"I know," she said, frowning. "I hate the added pressure this puts on both of you. You have enough on your plates. And with last week's theft of a horse at another ranch…"

Shane clenched his jaw. He'd just read an email from the

Emerald Ridge Police Department with more bad news and hated to worry his mother. But if she didn't find out from him, she'd find out from Rafe or Darla. Better from him.

He cleared his throat. "There's been another crime, this time at the Wellington Ranch."

His mother's eyes widened. "What happened?"

He read the email and summarized it for his mother. "Apparently their fence was sabotaged, and five cows escaped."

"You heard about it, too?" Rafe's voice interrupted them. "I was just coming to talk to you about it." He leaned down and kissed his mom's cheek. "Hi, Mom."

"Hi, honey."

"Were their security cameras disabled as well?" Rafe asked.

"I don't know," Shane said.

"These thieves need to be caught soon," Rafe muttered. "We don't need any more trouble than we've already got."

"Agreed." Shane looked at his watch. "I've got to run and pick up Brady."

"Half day today?" his mom asked.

"Yep. I told him he could come to the stables later and see the horses."

Shelley smiled wide. "Make sure you bring him by to see me, too."

"Of course." He hugged his mom and grabbed his Stetson. "We'll talk again later?" He caught Rafe's eye, and his brother nodded.

Twenty minutes later, he and Brady were back, his son talking a mile a minute about the new foal Shane was taking him to see. "Is the baby little? Is it bigger than me? Can I ride it?"

As they approached the entrance to the barn, Shane got down to Brady's level and took his son by the shoulders.

"Yes, she's little, but bigger than you. And no, you can't ride her, she's still a baby. Now, Mockingbird is very protective of her baby, so you have to be quiet and gentle, okay? No running and shouting."

Brady nodded, his eyes round. "Okay, Dad, I won't scare her."

Shane tried not to laugh as Brady tiptoed into the barn. He led his son to Mockingbird's stall.

"Hi, Mama," he said, his voice pitched low. He held out his hand, palm up, and Birdie came over and nuzzled him. "Can we see your beautiful baby?"

He gave Brady a carrot to feed Mockingbird and reminded him how to hold it properly. Brady giggled when the horse's lips tickled his fingers.

Having eaten her treat, Mockingbird moved out of the way, and Shane lifted Brady up on his shoulders so he could see the foal.

His son gasped. "She's so cute!"

The foal was pure black, like its mother, with big ears and gangly legs.

"What's her name?" Brady asked.

"Dilly," Shane said. "Like armadillo."

"That's a funny name. But she looks like a Dilly. Come here, Dilly."

The foal wandered over, and Brady gasped.

"She listened to me!"

Shane smiled. "I guess she likes you."

"Hi, Dilly-dilly. I'm Brady."

For the next few minutes, Shane watched the kid interact with the mare and foal. Brady was gentle, and Mockingbird seemed to understand that he was just a child. Dilly was curious, and stuck her nose between the bars, letting his son pet her while trying to get in some nibbles. Brady took it all in stride.

"Look at you," Garth said, voice booming as he strode down the aisle of the stable, the vet behind him. "Have you come to meet Dilly?"

Brady turned toward his grandfather and grinned. "She likes me!"

"I'll bet she does." Garth's voice was filled with pride.

Brady watched the vet examine Mockingbird and Dilly, peppering the patient woman with questions.

Garth leaned toward Shane and lowered his voice. "I think it's time that child had a horse of his own." He nodded toward Dilly. "Maybe this one."

Shane's spine stiffened. "I don't know, Dad. It's a lot of responsibility for a child."

"Nonsense. You three had horses growing up."

"Yes, but we lived on the ranch. Brady splits his time between me and Lacey. I'm not even sure how she feels about it."

"Well, you should find out. Six years old is the perfect time to start taking care of an animal."

Shane bristled. "Dad…"

"Oh, I recognize that 'Dad' tone," a female voice said.

Shane turned at Poppy's voice. His sister walked in, hugged Shane and their father, then nodded toward Brady.

"He's fallen in love with the foal, I see," she mused.

"Which is why he's the ideal age for a horse of his own," Garth reiterated.

Shane stared at Brady and the foal and mentally counted to ten. It would be better to keep silent and let the two of them make whatever plans they wanted. But at the end of the day, he was Brady's dad and had the ultimate say.

However, instead of arguing with him, Poppy looked at their dad, put a hand on his arm, and said, "Dad, *you* might think that. *I* might even agree with you. But let Shane decide."

"Thanks, Poppy, I—"

"Let Shane decide what?"

Shane closed his eyes in frustration as Rafe entered the barn.

"Rafe, this isn't what I had in mind when I said to you we'd talk later," Shane ground out.

"I know," he said, "but what are you talking about *now*?"

Rafe glanced among the three of them, and Shane briefly wondered what life as an only child might be like.

"Brady loves Dilly," Poppy explained. "Dad wants Brady to have a horse, Shane isn't sure, and I said that Dad has to let Shane decide."

"Oh, Brady definitely needs a horse," Rafe said.

"I'm getting a horse?" Brady asked, eyes bright. "Dad, really? Can I?"

Shane shot his family murderous looks before banking his anger and turning to his son. "We'll see, Brady. It's a lot of responsibility, and I'm not sure now is the right time."

"Please, Dad, *please*?"

"Brady." Shane made his voice stern. He didn't want to have a full-blown argument with anyone right now, but he needed the child to listen to him.

Brady exhaled a huge breath, like the weight of the world had slammed into him. "Okay." Drooping, he turned back to Dilly.

"Guys," Shane said to his family, "I appreciate all of you, but I don't like being ganged up on, and especially not in front of my son."

"You're right," Garth conceded. "I'm sorry."

Shane paused. While his dad wasn't a bad guy, he was opinionated and he rarely apologized. He had no idea what caused the change—actually, it was probably his mom and her moving out of, and then back into, the house—but whatever the cause, Shane appreciated it.

"I'm sorry, too," Poppy told him. "I shouldn't have butted in. I was just looking for Dad to see if he was willing to watch Joey while Leo and I have a date night."

Garth's face brightened. "Like I'd ever say no!"

"I'm sorry, too," Rafe said. "You're right. I should stick to my own business, which in this case was making sure we have a few gentle horses for today's riders. I was looking for Vivienne, and the family meeting distracted me."

Shane nodded to them all. "Thank you. Rafe, I'm pretty sure you've got some gentle ones, if I remember the list Raul showed me earlier, but check with him. Now, I've got to get Brady back to his mom and finish up my own work. Oh, and I haven't seen Viv."

Convincing a reluctant six-year-old to leave Dilly was challenging, but Shane managed it, bringing Brady back to Lacey's place. As he returned to his office, he shook his head at what had gone down in the barn. Jeez, with all their input about getting Brady his own horse, imagine how they'd react if he told them he was trying to improve his image. He laughed as he pictured his siblings and dad giving him a stack of papers filled with all the things he needed to work on to improve himself and find a wife. Good thing they didn't know about Naomi.

As he pulled his truck up to his office, he saw his cousin Micah.

Jumping out, he raised an arm to flag him down.

"Hey, there," he said, patting Micah on the back. "It's like a family reunion today."

"Oh? What's up?"

Shane shook his head. "No idea. But I've run into Mom, Dad, Poppy and Rafe. Rafe twice, actually. It's a good thing I like them all," he said with a laugh. Even if they got on his last nerve sometimes.

"Speaking of Poppy, how's baby Joey?"

"Adorable, as usual."

Micah nodded. "I never imagined one baby could stir up so much drama."

Shane sobered. "I know. I always thought my parents' marriage was perfect, but now I see the cracks, and I've gotta say, it shook me."

"Me, too. I really hope there's a happy ending with this one. Especially for Joey."

"Same."

"Anyway, that's not what I came here for," Micah said. "The fence line at the cattle ranch was sabotaged."

"Ours, too? I heard about the Wellingtons', but didn't realize we'd been hit, also. Did we lose anything?"

Micah shook his head. "No, but this has to stop. I was thinking of going undercover as a cowboy to catch the thief red-handed. What do you think?"

Pausing, Shane thought about it. As CEO of the cattle ranch operation, Micah was deeply involved, but outside of the office, he wasn't a recognizable face, especially not with the other ranch hands. He could probably get pretty far with an investigation, and more importantly, he was completely trustworthy.

"If you're up for it, I think it's a great idea. Not really up to me though."

"I'm gonna run it by Vivienne and Drake. Just wanted to see what you thought."

Shane shook his hand. "I like it. And if you need my

help with anything, just ask. Okay? Especially if it keeps you safe."

Micah grinned. "No cowboy moves for the cowboy. Got it."

Chapter Three

The next morning, Naomi went to her grandmother's apartment to help her clean for Passover before her lunch with Shane. Dressed in old jeans and a long-sleeved T-shirt, she carried her lunch outfit on a hanger, planning to change before she left.

"Hi, Bubbe." She kissed the older woman's soft cheek before hanging up her outfit in the hall closet.

"I can't believe you want to spend your morning with me," her grandmother said. "Don't you have better things to do with your time?"

"Absolutely not," Naomi said. "I love spending time with you, and with the holiday coming up, there's a lot to do. Especially since you're hosting the entire family. It's the perfect way to spend a morning."

Her grandmother looked at her askance. "You and I have very different ideas of perfect. However, I won't argue about getting to see my granddaughter. What's that?" Bubbe nodded toward the clothes in the closet as Naomi slid the door shut.

Naomi entered the kitchen. "My clothes for lunch with Shane. Want to start with your fridge?"

Her grandmother pressed her lips together. "That's right. Your fake date. Can't show up in your schleppy clothes."

Opening the freezer, Bubbe started pulling out a variety of frozen foods.

What in the world does one woman need with so much frozen food? Shaking her head, Naomi helped her empty the freezer out so they could clean it, noting the four types of frozen vegetables, six different frozen fruit combinations, three frozen vegetarian lasagnas and two frozen lamb curries. Aside from the amount of food, her grandmother ate way healthier than she did. Where was the ice cream, deep-dish pizza or bagels?

"It's a not a fake date, exactly. It's a test run to figure out what he's doing wrong. I told you, I'm not ready to date." Even if it *felt* like a fake date to her, something she'd never admit to her grandmother.

Bubbe sputtered and gave her the side eye. "And he's not Jewish."

Naomi stuck her head back in the freezer to quell the bright red inferno in her cheeks. Another reason why no matter how handsome he might be, she was going to resist his charms.

"True. But it doesn't matter because he needs to work on his dating image. How better to do that than for me to observe him at lunch?"

Oh, that sounded lame.

Bubbe handed her a fresh sponge with soap, and Naomi scrubbed the now empty freezer.

"It sounds suspiciously like a move a guy would make when he wants to ask out a girl but is too *nebishy* to actually do so."

Was she right? Naomi wrinkled her nose, as much from the cleanser smell as from curiosity. As she covered the bottom of the freezer with foil, she thought back to Shane's suggestion.

Seated across from him, staring into his solemn face, he'd appeared earnest in his desire for self-improvement. Was it all an act? He certainly wasn't a coward. Like all Fortune men, he exuded confidence. Then again, she didn't know him well. And in the years since their one date, it was obvious he'd changed. She'd have to see how he behaved today.

"I don't think so, Bubbe. I mean, he hired me. Signed a contract and everything. I don't think he'd go to that much trouble if all he wanted was to ask me out."

Even with the Fortune fortune.

"But it's one lunch," she continued. "I'll know more after we finish." She pointed to the pile of frozen food on the counter. "Do you really need all that?"

Her grandmother sorted through the food, tossing some and keeping the rest. Meanwhile, Naomi stretched out the kinks in her neck and moved on to the refrigerator. Passover cleaning was exhausting, and she was glad her grandmother was letting her help. To prepare for the upcoming holiday, the entire kitchen had to be turned over, pulling out special dishes, pots and pans and utensils, and doing a deep cleaning. It was too much for her grandmother to do at one time, so they started early and covered the clean surfaces with foil until the start of the holiday.

The mindless work gave Naomi time to think. Unfortunately, that enabled thoughts of her ex-boyfriend to enter her mind. Even six months after he cheated on her and dumped her, the rejection stung. Her chest still ached as images from that awful day played like a slideshow in her mind. He'd decided he wanted children—biological ones—and Naomi couldn't give them to him. His jawline had hardened, his lip had curled, and he'd ended his video breakup call, leaving her feeling worthless.

She shook her head. Therapy had taught her long ago she had value even if she couldn't bear children, but his behavior had put a chink in that armor of knowledge. She didn't want to be the person who equated a woman's value with the ability—or desire—to have children. She was intelligent and productive and worth something just because she breathed. She knew that. But recently, she'd needed a refresher. So she'd thrown herself into her work to keep herself distracted and to remind herself how worthwhile she was.

It had worked...until Shane walked into her office. His reemergence into her life brought with it confusion, embarrassment and...lust? She scoffed. Maybe she really did need to start dating again if the first handsome man to enter her office was going to make her insides melt.

Scrubbing the inside of the fridge, she reminded herself that Shane was a client, like anyone else. She wasn't about to fall for him, even if he had changed. Not after the way he'd treated her. This was business, that was all. And if the faults she found in him gave her a little satisfaction, well, she was human, right?

When the entire kitchen was spick-and-span and she'd restocked the refrigerator with kosher-for-Passover food on one shelf and regular items her grandmother would eat between now and the holiday on another shelf, she went off to change. Emerging from the bedroom cleaned up, dressed and made up, she draped the hanger with her previous cleaning outfit over her arm.

Her grandmother held her at arm's length and examined her.

"You look beautiful," she said. "If Shane doesn't think you're the most gorgeous woman alive, he's delusional."

Laughter bubbled in her chest. She smiled at her grandmother. "It's not a date, Bubbe, so he's not going to pay any attention to me or what I'm wearing. But thank you."

She smoothed her hands over her lightweight camel wool trousers and adjusted the hem of her burgundy sweater. Her grandmother adjusted its cowl neck.

"Love you," Naomi said.

"Love you, too. Now, go have fun on your non-date. He's gorgeous. Maybe you can use it as a test to see if you're ready to dip your toes back in the dating pool."

"Bubbe!"

Her grandmother cackled, and Naomi turned red once again—matching her top—but she had no time to stick her head in the freezer because Shane was due to pick her up any second.

"You're impossible." She gave the older woman a kiss and rushed outside. Since she was supposed to critique every aspect of Shane's behavior, he'd arranged to pick her up at her office, but when she realized she'd be at her grandmother's, he'd offered to pick her up here instead. His silver pickup truck pulled up to the curb just as she stepped onto the sidewalk.

"Game on," she whispered.

Shane met her on the passenger side.

"Hi." He opened the door and extended a hand to help her into the cab.

Dressed in black jeans and cowboy boots with a gray silk shirt beneath a gray sports coat, he reminded her of a model. One of those sexy cowboy models. Her belly fluttered.

"Hi." Her voice sounded breathless. Bubbe must have gotten under her skin more than she thought. While Shane shut the door and walked around the front of the truck to the driver's side, she took a moment to center herself.

Naomi Katz did not ruffle. She needed to remember that.

They made small talk on the short drive to the Emerald Ridge Hotel.

She pulled out her phone and noted her observations as they pulled up to the entrance of the grand hotel.

"You're taking notes?" Shane asked, lips quirking.

Naomi nodded. "If you want me to determine what you need to improve, or even what you do well, I have to. Does it make you uncomfortable?"

"No, I guess that makes sense," he answered.

They exited the truck and he handed his keys to the valet. He walked next to Naomi, his hand resting firmly on her lower back as they entered the hotel. Her back warmed to his touch. A few guests mingled in the ornate lobby and several waited for the dedicated elevator to take patrons to the penthouse floor of the hotel, where Captain's was located.

As he stood beside her, she stole admiring glances at him. He was tall and sleek and reminded her of a jaguar with his innate grace and coiled strength. He didn't fidget or move from one foot to the other, but stood tall and proud. He'd shaved, his face smooth with a hint of the dark whiskers along his jaw. His hair was slicked back, and he smelled…divine.

Her pulse raced. She shouldn't inhale. This was a business lunch, nothing more. But a woman had to breathe, right? And standing this close to him, heat radiated off his body, and his clean scent made her belly flutter even more than before. The arrival of the elevator shifted her focus, and she let out a breath of relief as they stepped inside before being whisked to the top floor of the hotel.

"Have you dined here before?" Shane asked as they walked across the marble foyer and into the restaurant.

Dark wood paneling on two sides of the restaurant, floor-to-ceiling windows on the third side, and mirrored shelves with top-shelf bottles of alcohol framed the space. Soft music played through hidden speakers, and wall sconces and fancy track lighting provided ambiance in this swanky seafood restaurant.

"Yes," she responded. She swallowed a lump in her throat. Her boyfriend had taken her here, back in the early days of their relationship when he'd been trying to impress her while home visiting her family. "It's one of my favorite special-occasion restaurants."

Or it used to be.

"Mine, too," he said. "I love their blackened Texas red-fish."

He pulled out her chair before sitting across from her, handing her the menu and then perusing the wine list.

"Do you prefer red or white?" he asked.

"White, please."

Naomi jotted down notes as he made all the right moves and said all the right things. They spent the next few minutes discussing wine pairings and favorite dishes, listening to specials and trying to decide what to order.

Finally, when he'd ordered his favorite—he laughed as he made fun of his inability to get past it on the menu—and she'd ordered Chilean sea bass, he sat back in his chair, one arm on the table, the other in his lap, and fixed his gaze on her.

Wow.

If this were an actual date, she'd be putty in his hands. Because when he looked at her like that, his dark blue eyes gleaming, his large hand resting comfortably on the table, his attention completely focused on her, she was tempted to fall.

Hard.

His conversation was entertaining, especially when he talked about Brady. His pride and adoration for his son shone as he relayed a funny situation at T-ball practice that happened last week. He also asked questions about Naomi's job and personal interests and responded with attentiveness to her.

As hard as she tried, she couldn't find anything wrong with his behavior.

In fact, if anyone was awkward, it was *her*.

She dropped the white linen napkin on the floor, and he rushed to pick it up for her. Wincing, she had to force herself to stay in the here and now, rather than follow her thoughts as they drifted back to her date with him years ago.

Or worse, wonder what it would be like to date him now.

"So, tell me," he said. "What made you decide to become an image consultant?"

A lot of people asked her this, so she had her stock answer ready. But for some reason, when Shane posed the question, she wanted to tell him more.

"I was always the one people came to for advice when I was growing up. Whether it was how to ask someone out, or break up with someone, what to wear on a date, or how to talk to a teacher, my friends turned to me. In college, while I was pursuing a business degree, friends and other students wanted my help crafting emails, polishing résumés or giving speeches. After I graduated, I worked in a marketing firm in Dallas for a short time, but I realized I wanted to help people, rather than companies. So, I took what I liked, combined it with what I was good at, and started my own firm."

She should have taken notes on Shane's way of asking questions and listening. Instead, she got lost in the admiration that radiated from his eyes, and how it filled her with pride. Mentally, she shook it off.

Or tried to.

"And how about you?" she asked. "What's it like to work in the family business?"

Now it was his turn to glow with pride.

"It's great," he said. "Frustrating as heck, because, you know, family."

She laughed.

"But I'm surrounded with people whom I love and care about, and who feel the same way about me."

"Even the…dare I say it…feud?"

Shane shrugged. "That feud among the Fortunes, Wellingtons and Leonettis is more of an older generation thing. The Fortunes and Wellingtons began their feud when a Fortune groom left a Wellington bride at the altar a century ago. She was humiliated, and the Fortune family presented the Wellingtons with a $1000 bottle of Leonetti wine as an apology. Unfortunately, that bottle was skunked—no one knew how—and that brought them into the feud, too. At this point, though, we all get along, especially since my sister Poppy is now engaged to Leo Leonetti. They're actually fostering baby Joey together. So it's more of a family story told when our parents get nostalgic. All the cousins get along. And even my dad and uncle, who bicker a lot, are each other's staunchest supporters when it comes to family."

The more she talked with Shane, the more conflicted she became. On the one hand, she'd been looking forward to finding fault with the man. It was mean of her, she knew, but after he dumped her and got engaged so soon after their date, a part of her would have gotten satisfaction out of finding a major flaw in his dating technique. But on the other hand, she wasn't about to sabotage her professionalism out of revenge. And from what she could see, there wasn't a thing wrong with him. In fact, she was starting to enjoy his company.

That *wouldn't* do.

She froze. As far as anyone in town knew, she was in a long-distance relationship. No one knew it had ended, and flirting with Shane would be a terrible look. Not to mention, it might encourage something she probably wasn't ready for.

Andrew's betrayal still hurt. More than she'd let on, even to her grandma. Even now, dread pressed down on her shoulders and a pit formed in her stomach when she thought about it. She thought the two of them had a future together. While everyone had talked about how hard a long-distance relationship could be, she and Andrew had figured out a way to make it, if not easy, workable. And the nights when she'd ached to be with him, they'd talked it through and had grown closer. At least she thought they had. Their breakup made her question everything. Especially her self-worth. He'd chosen someone else, someone who could give him the children she couldn't. Her body had betrayed not only her, but her ability to have a relationship with him. And although the soul-crushing initial hurt had passed, she was wary of starting something new. How would she ever trust someone again if she'd been so wrong the first time?

And, besides, Shane was her client.

"How's your grandmother?" Shane's question drew her attention back to the present.

"Feisty as ever," she replied. "I was just over there this morning helping her get ready for Passover."

He smiled. "I'll bet she loves having you around."

"It's mutual. I always adore spending time with her. But since my parents are away on a cruise, I've stopped by even more frequently. She's my favorite person in the world."

"That must be nice," he said. "She's lucky to have you."

"I'm sure you can relate," she murmured. "You have your siblings and cousins living on the same property as you."

He laughed. "Don't forget we grew up in the same house."

Naomi shook her head. "How in the world did that work?"

"It was fun," he said. "It was like having a family reunion every day."

"What about the lack of privacy?" As an only child, she couldn't imagine never having time to herself, no matter how much she'd wished for a brother or sister when she was growing up.

He cocked an eyebrow. "You've seen the monstrosity of a house we grew up in. Even with all of us under one roof, the two families had their own wings. We all had our own bedrooms, and there was plenty of privacy when we needed it."

She wouldn't call the place a monstrosity. Ridiculously huge, maybe. Inconceivably luxurious, definitely. But a monstrosity?

He clearly wasn't overly impressed with his family's wealth. A flush of adrenaline rushed through her.

"Although now that our families are expanding, it's nice to have our own homes," he added. "Did you hear Leo and Poppy are fostering the baby left on their doorstep?"

Naomi warmed. Anything relating to adoption or foster care interested her. Between her friends' texts and gossip in town, she'd heard the outline of the story. It gave her hope for her own journey one day.

"I think what she's doing is wonderful."

His expression relaxed. "I do, too, *now*, but you'd be surprised how stressful it's been." He lowered his voice. "What with first thinking my dad might be Joey's father, watching the toll that possibility took on my parents' marriage, and then seeing how attached Poppy got to the baby only to fear having him taken away when the DNA results came back. But she spoke to Social Services recently, and they told her she and Leo could continue to foster the baby since the investigation into who the baby is has gone nowhere."

Naomi's heartbeat quickened with envy. "Poppy must be so happy. She adores that little guy." She crossed her arms over her stomach, longing for a baby of her own.

"She does." He looked out the windows at the expansive views of Emerald Ridge. In the distance was Fortune land, more than three thousand acres. That land was filled with family history. Families stuck together, no matter what. "I can't help wondering who the mother is, and how she could just abandon a baby," he said.

Her heart swelled. "I know I never could." If she were ever lucky enough to have children of her own, she'd keep them close and make sure they knew they were loved.

A flush crept over his high cheekbones. He cleared his throat. "About that... I never meant to make you uncomfortable, back when we went out that time. I don't know what I was thinking, asking you to tell me a secret. And then just saying why not adopt, like it was all no big deal."

She swallowed. "Actually, you're the first person who made me think it was okay to consider adoption. And seeing how accepting your family is about Joey... Well, it gives me hope."

A look of relief crossed his face and silence stretched between them. He shook his head, making circles on the tablecloth as he spoke. "I really thought my parents' marriage was over." Looking up at her, pain lurked in his blue eyes. "I mean, how do you get past the love of your life fathering another woman's baby? And even though it turned

out to be false, there are certain things that can't be un-
done, you know?"

A desire to reach for his hand came over her, and it
took all of her restraint not to physically comfort him. "It's
tough," she said softly. "It's like trying to stuff toothpaste
back into the tube. Luckily, they didn't have to find out."

She clenched her hands in her lap, the stress of keeping
secrets weighing on her. Garth was working on his marriage as they spoke, and a newfound well of sympathy for
both him and Shane filled her. There were so many people affected by one little baby. Unfortunately, even though
she knew a lot about how hard Garth was working to improve his marriage, she couldn't say anything to Shane.
Her chest ached from sadness. She had to be careful not to
give away anything.

"Hopefully your parents will come out stronger after all
of this is over," she added. "And it's probably one of those
times where having lots of family around is a help."

His expression cleared. "I think you're right. There are
always people to offer advice and perspective. It's one of
the reasons I want a big family in the future."

Another ache rolled through Naomi, but this time, the
reason surprised her. Maybe it was all the talk about Poppy
and Joey. Maybe it was Shane's easy acceptance of the baby.
Or maybe it was his clear love for his son, but an urge to
offer herself as a match overtook her.

Her breath quickened with fear. Shane and she were a
bad idea. And turning this personal would risk their business relationship, maybe even force her to lose Shane as
a client.

Still, the notion of finding him a "perfect match" filled
her mouth with bitterness, and she took a large gulp of
wine. Did she really want to help him find someone *else* to

possibly marry? What if the two of them were the perfect match, and she was self-sabotaging because of her memories of one lousy date years ago?

"No wonder you and your boyfriend are able to make a long-distance relationship work," Shane said. "You make everyone around you feel like everything will work out." He smiled at her, and her heart lurched.

She tried to respond, but came up blank.

Maybe she should tell him about Andrew after all. He'd given her the perfect lead-in. People broke up all the time, right? She could even casually mention she was back on the market...

"Another reason why I'm glad I hired you," Shane continued.

Shocked back to reality, she buried the desire to confess to a breakup. He wanted her to help him find a girlfriend. He didn't want *her*. If she told him she'd lost her boyfriend, he might doubt her abilities.

The idea didn't sit well with her. She always told her clients to be honest about themselves. Vulnerabilities made people human.

But she'd already confessed one of her biggest to him—that she couldn't have children—and although he'd reacted well, he'd still decided to pursue his crush instead of her. She didn't want to push her luck and lose the business relationship.

Besides, she needed to maintain professionalism. She'd take what attracted her to him and help Shane use it to his advantage with other women. Even if it turned her stomach a little to do so.

"Oh, maybe I shouldn't have said that." A look of concern crossed his face. "I didn't mean to make you sound like an escort."

She choked on her wine, straightened in her chair, eyes wide. "That didn't even occur to me," she said.

He closed his eyes, his neck flushing above his collar. "I really stepped in it, didn't I?"

He hadn't *really* called her an escort, had he? No one could mess up that badly, right? She took a deep breath and threw back her shoulders. "Don't worry about it. I'll let it slide this time."

Leaning toward her, he reached for her hand. His palm was warm, his grasp firm. He squeezed her fingers. Heat zipped along her arm.

"I'm truly sorry. I did not mean to offend you, and I apologize for my clumsy speech."

Speech? Words? All she could think about was his touch. The tiny hairs on her arm rose, and her breath left her lungs. She blinked.

"It's really okay."

He pulled his hand away and knocked into her water glass, which tipped and spilled all over her lap.

She gasped.

Rushing around the table, he tried to blot up the mess, patting at her lap. His hands were everywhere they shouldn't be, and she pushed him away even as desire pooled in her belly. He jerked and bumped his head into her cheekbone.

"Ow!" She raised a hand to the side of her face, just as the waiter appeared with their check.

"Is everything okay?" he asked, surveying the scene, eyebrow raised.

"She needs another napkin," Shane said. "And some ice?"

Naomi shook her head. "Just the napkin. Or two." She grabbed Shane's arm to prevent his continued patting of her lap. "I'm fine. Really. Just go sit back down."

"I'm sorry," he said. "Again. Man." He shook his head. "I

can't wait to see the report you draw up about this. I swear this has never happened to me before."

"I must bring out the worst in you," she teased, smiling in spite of herself.

Stifling a laugh, he pulled out his wallet and handed his credit card to the waiter.

"You don't need to pay for lunch," she said. "This is business."

"After everything I did? It's my treat, and I won't hear any arguments about it."

She wanted to say he sounded like his father, but refrained just in time. Instead, she nodded. "Fine. Thank you."

She tapped her foot, eager to get back to her office and change her clothes. Not to mention, put some distance between herself and Shane. She smoothed her hands again over her trousers, shifting uncomfortably as the damp fabric touched her skin. Thank goodness she kept an extra pair of clothes in the office.

The waiter returned, and Shane signed the bill with a flourish. She frowned. The motion was out of character for what she expected from him, although she couldn't pinpoint why. Grabbing her phone, she made a few more notes and rose when he came around and pulled out her chair.

"I assume you're ready to leave," he said, his voice rueful.

"I could do with a change of clothing." She smiled as she walked with him to the elevator.

They stepped inside, and she stared at the light as it started to descend. Ten, nine, eight. Suddenly, the elevator jerked to a stop. The doors made a grinding sound and remained shut.

Naomi met Shane's gaze, eyes wide.

"That didn't sound good," she said. Her throat tightened,

and her heart rate increased. She took deep breaths to try to remain calm.

"No, it didn't. Looks like we're stuck inside this elevator."

Chapter Four

Shane pressed the call button, and a moment later, a voice responded.

"Hello?"

"Hi, we're trapped," he said.

Naomi gripped the strap of her purse, trying not to panic as the elevator techs responded. "Yeah, we're aware. The elevator should be repaired shortly. Hang tight."

"Hang tight?" Naomi murmured. "That's all he had to say?"

"Maybe another potential client?" Shane joked.

She shook her head. "I'm not sure how you can laugh about this. We're stuck in a box that could crash down any moment."

"Hey." Shane stepped forward and placed his hands on her shoulders. The minty-pine scent of his aftershave wafted around her. "We're going to be fine. It's probably some minor repair that will take a couple minutes. Like a button that has to be pushed."

"Minor? Did you hear the grinding sound?" Her voice trembled.

"I did." He slid his hands from her shoulders to her upper arms, squeezing gently, sending spirals of heat up and down her arms. "It's going to be okay. I promise."

"But how do you know?" Naomi hated sounding this unsure, but between navigating lunch with Shane and now being trapped in an elevator—something she'd always feared—her nerves were shot.

"I'm a Fortune," he said. "We know things."

He straightened, giving himself such a snobby air that she couldn't help but laugh. The burst of air from her lungs relieved some of the pressure inside her.

"There you go," he soothed. "Are you afraid of riding elevators or are you claustrophobic?"

Naomi stepped away from him and rolled her shoulders. "I'm not claustrophobic. I'm afraid of broken elevators that might fall eight or so floors and crush us to death."

Leaning against the wall, he crossed his feet at the ankles and rested his hands on the bar. Then nodded. He cut a dashing figure, and Naomi swallowed.

"I can understand that," he said gently. "But they're going to get us out of here."

She prayed he was right.

He glanced at his watch and frowned. "Soon, I hope. I've got to pick Brady up from school."

"What time does school let out?"

"Two o'clock." He pulled his phone out of his pocket. "Great, no service."

Naomi checked her phone. "Me neither."

Worry crossed his face. "I'm not going to be able to call the school and let them know I'll be late."

Sympathy made her chest constrict. He'd been kind to her, and she wanted to make him feel better, too. "Maybe the guy on the other end of the call box can help you out, if it comes to that."

He looked dubiously at the control panel. "Maybe."

She also didn't like not being able to reach people, especially her grandmother. But dwelling on that wouldn't help.

"You're really involved in Brady's life," she remarked.

"Of course I am." He frowned again, looking at her like she'd sprouted a second head or something. "I'm his dad. No matter what problems Lacey and I might have had as a couple, I'd never let anything stand in the way of my being with my son." He rolled his eyes. "Except possibly an elevator."

"How often is he with you?"

"Officially, we have a fifty-fifty split, but he's free to come and go as he pleases, and we each take up the slack when the other needs it." He exhaled a frustrated breath. "His mom has an appointment today for her wedding, so I said I'd get him from school."

Her eyes widened. "Oh, wow, she's getting remarried?"

He nodded. "Yep. Great guy. Brady loves him." He chuckled. "In fact, he thinks I should get remarried, now, too. You know, so we can be equal. He gave me lots of tips for meeting women."

Naomi smiled. Her heart squeezed. This man was such a good father. "Anything useful?"

Shrugging, he replied, "Depends on how you feel about LEGO bricks."

He looked around and gave a wry chuckle. "Can't wait to hear what he'll say about the elevator getting stuck."

Naomi shifted, her cheeks warming. Was he flirting with her? By now they were both sitting on the floor next to each other. There was only about an inch or two separating them. Awareness of his proximity filled her thoughts, putting her on hyper-alert.

Or maybe it was just her nerves about the elevator.

"How old is he, six?"

Shane nodded.

"Well, then, he'll probably tell you that you should have fixed the elevator yourself to impress me."

"Is that what I have to do to impress you?"

He looked at her sideways, and her cheeks heated. Now, *that* was flirting.

"It definitely would be on the right track."

His mouth twitched, and he rose, examined the control panel, then sat down again. But this time, his leg touched hers.

Heat from the contact zipped up her leg toward her core.

He leaned toward her. "Guess I'll have to find some other way."

His gravelly voice made her insides somersault. The air around them electrified. In the silence, their breathing was magnified. His hand rested on his leg, and she stared at it, almost willing it to touch her.

What would that feel like? He'd already touched her shoulders and upper arms, but how would his palm feel against her cheek? Or her neck?

Just thinking about it made goose bumps rise at her nape. She shivered.

"Are you cold?" His deep voice curled around her, making her want to lean into him.

"No," she whispered. She cleared her throat. "No." This time, her voice was louder.

She turned her head and admired his profile. Strong nose, square jaw, curly dark hair. Its tips brushed the top of his collar. Her fingers ached to run through it.

Just as the thought entered her head, he turned.

Now they were face-to-face.

She should avert her gaze or get up to examine the control box. Maybe there was something *she* could do to fix the elevator.

But his blue eyes pinned her in place. The pulse at his temple throbbed. He blinked, and now he was looking at her mouth.

She bit her lip, and his pupils dilated. They couldn't kiss. She was supposedly in a relationship, and he was her client.

His lips parted a fraction. What would they feel like on her mouth? She opened her mouth to protest, to say anything that might return them back to normal, but nothing came out. His eyes darkened to a navy blue. Dark lashes framed them. His nose was a little crooked... She was playing with fire. But the thought of pulling away was beyond her. Or maybe *she* was doing something to draw him closer.

Either way, they were barely a breath apart. Her eyelids fluttered. He was going to kiss her. She should turn away, but why? What was the harm of one kiss?

Wasn't there some rule about whatever happened in a stuck elevator stayed in a stuck elevator? If not, there should be.

That was it—if he didn't kiss her in two more seconds, she was going to kiss him, relieve this agony and to heck with the consequences.

A groan, followed by the elevator jerking to life, made them scramble away from each other. It began to descend. Naomi got up and smoothed her clothes. Heart still hammering in her chest, she watched as Shane reached for his hat and cleared his throat. The elevator jolted to a stop, the doors opened, and the maintenance crew greeted them, asking after their health. With an awkward nod and half smile, she escaped the elevator and stepped into the lobby first.

The bright sunshine after the close quarters of the elevator brought reality crashing back. Not only had she almost kissed him, but now she had to drive back with him.

No way. She couldn't do it. She looked at her watch.

"Shane."

He stopped moving toward the front doors.

"If you leave now, you'll make it back in time to pick up Brady."

"I'll drop you off first."

She shook her head. "No, that will make you late. Really, go ahead. I promise I'm fine. I'd like to get some air after the elevator, anyway."

"Are you sure?" He looked conflicted, but there was no way she was getting into his truck.

"Go. You'll be late," she urged.

With a nod, he turned and strode out of the hotel.

And for the first time in what felt like hours, Naomi breathed.

Shane opened and closed his hands on the steering wheel, trying to loosen some of the tension as he drove to pick up his son. The short drive from Emerald Ridge to Brady's elementary building passed without him noticing the magnolia trees beginning to bud, the flowers dotting the hills with color or the warm breeze blowing through the open window of his truck. His mind spun in a million different directions, bouncing from his lunch to the elevator to his flirting to his son. If thoughts were Ping-Pong balls, his skull would be bruised.

He'd tried so hard during lunch to act naturally so that Naomi could evaluate him. But somewhere along the way, he'd started thinking of her less as an image consultant and more as a date. She was beautiful, sure, but so easy to talk to. They had things in common, and being with her had felt right. He could picture her fitting into his life. And then, as soon as he'd mentioned her boyfriend, everything had gone south.

As soon as the words left his mouth, though, jealousy struck. He'd gone hot and cold. He'd wanted her to say she would break up with the guy.

Imagine, he actually wanted to ruin a relationship!

It was a good thing he hadn't said anything. It was one thing to be awkward, it was an entirely different thing to break up a relationship. He could only imagine the dings he'd get in her report. He was *not* that guy. His heart pounded against his rib cage. The awkwardness he'd hoped he'd outgrown was still there. How could one woman do this to him, and why couldn't it be a woman who was available? Embarrassment overtook him.

Spilling the water on her must have been some kind of portent of what was to come. Not only had his clumsiness probably merited an entire paragraph in her report, but it led to more discomfort between the two of them. Once again, he was back to his old ways around women. And the elevator? He ran a hand over his eyes, then quickly returned it to the steering wheel as he pulled up to Brady's school. He'd flirted with her, almost kissed her. And he'd have sworn she flirted right back. Which couldn't possibly have happened. He'd obviously misread the signals. She never would have done that if she were attached.

Which she was.

He must have just gotten caught up in her fear. Yeah, that was it. Stuck elevators scared her, and he'd swooped in to save her. Apparently, he had a hero complex. Just great. He wouldn't be surprised if she emailed him to tell him she was dropping him as a client.

But, oh, her lips had beckoned him. Had they been stuck

five minutes longer, he'd have tasted them, teased them between his teeth...

Brady climbed into the truck.

"Hi, Dad, I got my spelling test back today." Beaming, he held it out, and Shane blinked away images of Naomi's mouth. He forced himself to focus on his son and the paper fluttering in his grasp.

"A perfect score. Way to go, kiddo!"

"What did you do today, Dad?"

Oh boy. Shane ran a hand through his hair

"Actually, I got caught in an elevator."

Brady's eyes widened. "Really?" Leave it to a six-year-old to think that was cool.

Shane gave his son the watered-down version. Although seat belted in place, Brady bounced up and down in his seat.

"You did it, Dad, you did it!"

"Not really. I didn't have anything to do with fixing the elevator."

"But you made the lady feel safe, right?"

That was one way of looking at it.

"And you protected her?"

She probably needed more protection *from* him rather than *by* him. "Uh, I guess."

"So, you're like a superhero! She'll definitely want to marry you now!"

It was all Shane could do not to crash his truck into the ditch on the side of the road. His arm swung out to keep Brady in place, even though the seat belt was more than sufficient.

"Marry me?"

"Yeah. Remember how we talked about you looking for a wife the other day? She'll totally want to marry you after how you protected her."

He didn't think she'd want to speak to him again, much less see him. Never mind marry him.

For a split second, his mind carried him away to what it would be like to marry someone like her. He smiled.

"See, you know I'm right, Dad."

Shane pulled into his ex-wife's driveway and put the truck into Park. "Unfortunately, Brady, she's already dating someone. And it wouldn't be right to steal her from another guy."

His son slumped in his seat. "No, stealing is wrong." Then he suddenly perked up. "But I don't think you should give up yet. Superheroes never give up."

"They also don't push people to do things they don't want to do." He ruffled Brady's hair. "Don't worry, bud, I'll find someone to marry when the time is right."

Shane gave him a kiss and helped him down from the truck before watching as the little boy ran into the house. He waved to the babysitter and pulled out of the driveway.

He'd bet money Brady was going to regale Lacey and Kevin with lots of stories about needing to find Shane a wife. He shook his head. He'd have to send his apologies.

Shane swore under his breath. He also owed Naomi an apology for stepping over boundaries. Regardless of her job, she hadn't signed on to flirting with him. And maybe, if he owned up to his mistakes he wouldn't get dinged as much in her report as if he left well enough alone. Punching her number into his phone, he prepared himself to talk to her.

Disappointment slithered down his spine when her voicemail answered. He sighed.

"Hey, Naomi, it's Shane Fortune. Listen, I wanted to make sure you were okay after the elevator and to apologize for my behavior at lunch today. It won't happen again."

Hanging up, he hoped it would be enough.

* * *

Finally back in her office later that day, Naomi released a huge breath, rolled her shoulders and tried to center herself. But her lunch had been…*unexpected*…and her normal methods of relaxing didn't work. Even the walk back hadn't cleared her mind as much as she'd hoped.

"Naomi," she said out loud, "you haven't made it this far professionally by allowing yourself to be distracted by good-looking men."

She thrust her shoulders back. "You've worked with celebrities and didn't get starstruck." She cleared her throat. "You're better than this. Now, get ahold of yourself and get to work."

Having given herself a good talking to, she had no choice but to listen. She put her phone on silent, forwarded her notes to her computer and dropped into her seat.

For the next hour, she forced herself to think about the lunch minus how attractive Shane was. And she didn't allow herself to think about the elevator. Nope, for her current purpose, that penthouse-level restaurant was on the ground floor. No small-box-filled-with-sexy-man thoughts at all.

It would have worked.

It *should* have worked.

Except for one problem.

Shane, himself.

He was perfect.

She scoffed. He wasn't perfect. No one was. And she had plenty of experience with his imperfections. But he'd been a perfect gentleman all through lunch, from the moment he picked her up until just before spilling the water on her. And even that wasn't awful. Sure, it was wet. She'd had to change her clothes the moment she'd entered her office in order to get rid of the clammy dampness against her skin. But it wasn't a deal-breaker.

If she'd been on an actual date with the man, she'd have been willing to see him again. Especially with how apologetic he'd been afterward.

The conk on the head? She ran her hand over it. No lump. Okay, the man was clumsy. But even gorgeous men could act like klutzes occasionally.

If she *were* to have a crush on him, his klutziness would keep him human.

She squinted at her computer screen, hoping miraculous inspiration would pop into her head. The first part of the report was easy. She liked to sandwich her criticism with a summary of all the things he'd done right. Her fingers flew across the keyboard as she enumerated his excellent manners, invigorating conversational skills, charm, charisma, and exceptional command of the menu.

Now came the hard part. Had his faults really been *that* bad? Would another woman, a woman he was dating, object to the same things she did? She wrinkled her brow, never having had this concern about a client before. She didn't want to risk her professionalism.

Just because she could forgive the water and the head bump, would someone else?

She needed to review her positive comments. Maybe she'd been *too* positive. Her stomach clenched as she re-read her introduction. She removed a few adjectives. But she knew she couldn't punish him for doing something well.

Her grandmother's voice entered her mind, reminding her she'd had no problem with other handsome clients. So what was her issue with Shane?

Did she want him to be more than a client?

Her stomach fluttered.

No, he couldn't be. She'd been burned before, by someone who should have been a perfect match. Her history with Shane and their different religions made it too hard. Not to mention, he was a Fortune, and that was a big deal in Emerald Ridge.

She needed a break. Pushing away from her desk, she grabbed her phone out of her bag.

Shane had left her a voicemail.

His deep voice left a small smile on her face, like an imprint, and she shivered at its vibrant tone. He was apologizing.

Warmth flooded through her. He was so sweet. She looked over at the powder room, where her wet clothes hung until she could bring them home. How thoughtful of him to call her and leave a message.

Honestly, it wasn't a big deal. Sure, it had been a shock, and a momentary sliver of embarrassment had struck her—along with a small amount of pain when his head collided with hers—but accidents happened. And he'd handled it with such aplomb afterward, she really couldn't fault him. She'd have to make special note in his report about that, so he didn't stress over it.

His apology gave her renewed focus and purpose, and allowed her to dive back into the critique. Still, it was difficult to separate out her personal feelings from the professional evaluation, and finally, after another hour, she gave up. Instead, she returned Shane's call.

"Hi, Shane, it's Naomi. It appears we're playing phone tag. I got your message. Please don't worry about it. Honestly, it didn't even register. Talk to you later."

She looked at her watch and decided to go home to start her own Passover prep. Grabbing her clothes from the powder room, she left.

Just pulling into her driveway lessened the tension she'd felt all day. She loved her house. It was small and neat, with bright red shutters and weathered clapboard. A few scrub pines grew in the yard, and in the distance, she could see part of the Fortune ranch.

Inside, she threw her wet clothes in the laundry room, kicked off her shoes and made a beeline for the pantry. She pulled out an open box of Cocoa Krispies and tossed a handful in her mouth. The chocolatey sugar gave her a jolt, and immediately, things looked better.

She was a sucker for sugary cereal.

After scrubbing out her fridge, she ran the dishwasher and moved her everyday dishes out of the way, replacing them with paper until the holiday arrived. And then she prepared a vegetable kugel for herself. Although she'd spend the seder with her grandmother, she still had seven days of Passover, and she needed foods to eat at home. As usual, she prepared herself lots of sweet snacks. Her sweet tooth was ravenous, especially during this holiday—jellied fruit, almond kisses, chocolate-covered matzah—and she made sure to stock enough to munch on throughout the entire seven days. Exhausted from her full day and ricocheting emotions, she fell into an exhausted sleep.

The following day, she returned to her grandmother's apartment to help her polish the silver and clean the second oven. Luckily, it was a nice day out, so once the oven was set to self-clean, they opened the windows wide and enjoyed the outside air rather than the chemical smell. Sitting next to her bubbe polishing the candlesticks, like she'd done with her every year, was a ritual Naomi treasured.

"So how was your lunch with Shane?" her grandmother asked.

And just like that, peace evaporated.

"It was fine."

She looked at Naomi over the rims of her silver glasses. "Tell me about it."

Without giving too much away about her client, she described the restaurant and the food. "Have you been there?" she asked.

"I was there when it first opened," Bubbe said. "I went with a few ladies from my bridge club. Very fancy. He picked quite a nice place for a trial run."

"It's still fancy, and the sea bass was amazing. When Mom and Dad come back from their vacation, we should go for a birthday or something," Naomi said.

Bubbe shrugged. "We can if you'd like. Personally, I don't need anything that fancy. As long as my family is together, I'm happy."

Naomi hugged her, inhaling her floral L'Air du Temps scent that was her signature perfume. "We'll all be together for the seder," she promised. "Mom and Dad will be jet-lagged, but here, as will the cousins and aunts and uncles."

Her grandmother's face brightened with joy. "I can't wait to see everyone." She turned to the pile of cookbooks on her dining table. "I've got my menu set and my grocery lists ready. We'll go shopping next week?"

Naomi nodded. "I can take care of it if you want."

"I'm not an invalid, *bubbelah*. We can go together."

"I know, sorry."

Her grandmother's face transformed, and a wicked gleam put Naomi on guard. "Should I invite Shane to join us?"

"Bubbe!"

The woman cackled, and Naomi shook her head. "You're impossible. I told you, we're not dating. He's my client."

"I think you're protesting a little too much," Bubbe said.
"I call it like I see it," she said.

Naomi sighed and continued cleaning in silence.

"What are you thinking?" her grandmother asked.

Despite the teasing, the older woman was her confidante. Anytime she'd ever had problems in her love life, Bubbe had been the first one she'd told. She always gave good advice and never betrayed her trust.

"When we were trapped in the elevator, Shane was so worried about missing his son's pickup from school. It's not that I wanted him to be anxious, but his obvious love for his son is everything I'd feel in his position. If I ever get married, I want a husband who is as devoted to our kids as Shane is toward his."

Her grandmother continued polishing, letting the silence build between them.

"Of course, I don't know if I'll ever get married or adopt children, so I'm not sure why I'm thinking about it." She swallowed. "I guess it was just a nice surprise to see Shane so invested."

"You're a healthy woman, and you recognize good qualities in a man when you see them," Bubbe said. "You'll have the family you want someday. Your ex-boyfriend was an idiot."

Naomi started to protest, but her grandmother held out her hand to stop.

"Let me finish, Naomi. I'm not saying he didn't have good qualities, but overall, he was a schmuck. I'm glad you're coming out of your funk, or as you young people say, moving through your stages of grief, but I hope you know that it's completely possible to find a man as devoted to his family as you are."

"I do," Naomi said. "Or I'm trying to."

"Good. Just be careful. Shane is gorgeous and kind and right in front of you. Be prepared. I don't want to see you hurt again…"

Naomi rolled her eyes and said, "Yes, Bubbe," sounding like a robot.

She paused. Her grandmother was the one person she could be completely honest with. "I'm afraid that I'll never find someone who can look past my infertility."

"What Andrew did to you was terrible, but not all men are like that. Still…"

Her grandmother's silence made her heart sink.

"Still what?"

"It couldn't hurt to slow things down a little. To give a lot of thought before you get too far into anything with Shane."

A ringtone interrupted them.

"Excuse me, Bubbe. Let me see who it is."

Shane. Speak of the devil.

"I've got to take this," she continued, rising from the table and walking toward the living room. "Hi, Shane, how are you?"

"Good. I was wondering if you'd be willing to come over for dinner tomorrow night?"

Naomi paused, looking back at her grandmother's profile in the other room.

"Um—"

He cut her off. "I've got Brady tomorrow night, and I thought it would be helpful if you met him, so that you could get an idea as to the type of stepmother I'd want to have."

She frowned. That seemed like an odd request. Not that wanting the right kind of woman to be a stepmother was so odd, but…if she wasn't so sure she and Shane were not meant to be together, she'd think he was looking for an excuse to see her.

"Unless you're busy tomorrow," he continued.

With a start, she realized she'd let the silence go on too long.

"No, I'm not busy, and if you think it would help for me to meet Brady, I'd be happy to come over for dinner."

The curious part of her was interested in seeing what kind of a child Shane was raising.

"And actually, I can bring over my report from our lunch and go over it with you."

He cleared his throat. "Should I be nervous about what you found?"

His deep voice held a hint of uncertainty in it, and another chink in her Shane armor appeared.

"No, you shouldn't. You'll see when I show it to you that I thought the lunch went well, and I have a few suggestions to make it even better when it's the real thing. But we can discuss all of that tomorrow. What time should I come over?"

"I'll pick you up at six. And let me guess, *don't spill water* is at the top of the list." Relief softened his tone.

"Ha!" She smile despite herself. "But there's no reason for you to pick me up. You're making dinner and you've got Brady. I'll drive myself."

Shane sighed. "I suppose that makes sense."

"Great, then I'll see you tomorrow."

She disconnected the call and returned to her grandmother. When she relayed the conversation, the woman smirked.

"Another fake date, huh?"

"Bubbe."

But she couldn't protest too much because her grandmother's thoughts echoed her own. Her pulse quickened with anticipation, but she tried to calm herself and lower her expectations. As odd as the invitation seemed to her, Shane sounded serious. Brady was his life. Anyone he dated had to accept that. And if her meeting the boy would help him find the perfect potential stepmother, then dinner all together made sense.

The only thing worse than repeating the mistakes of the past—being a pseudo-date until his next real love interest came along—was to not recognize that potential and show too much eagerness. Because that would be humiliating, and she wasn't about to do that to herself. No, she'd have to tread carefully with Shane. And Brady.

Chapter Five

Driving onto the Fortune ranch always knocked Naomi off balance. If she didn't already know the Fortunes were a big deal, entering the family side of the ranch convinced her. As her Jeep made its way up the long gravel drive, she passed the ostentatious main house where Garth, Shelley, Hayden and Darla lived. The large main ranch house was a sprawling castle-like home with stately peaked towers in the center and large wings on either side. White stucco and huge windows, as well as ornate molding let everyone who entered the wrought-iron gates know that this was a prosperous family ranch. About a mile down the road, and then spaced about a quarter mile apart, were each of the six cousins' homes, mini versions of the main house, minus the wings.

Poppy's home was the first on the right, surrounded by trees for privacy. She'd visited her friend there many times. However, ever since Shane had dropped her for someone else, whenever she visited Poppy, she'd kept her head down, hoping to avoid any sign of Shane for fear of awkwardness or embarrassment. Despite the vast size of the ranch— about three thousand acres—she'd been wary of visiting too often.

But now that she was working for Shane, that wariness

disappeared. She satisfied her curiosity by slowing as she passed each of the cousins' homes, unconcerned about who she might see. Similar in size and shape, each home reflected the individual preferences of the homeowner. So why it came as a shock that Shane's practically screamed "family man," she didn't know.

Like the others, his home was white stucco, with a massive dark wood door and a circular turret of windows. But in the front yard, a swing hung from one of the trees and a huge outdoor play set with slides, climbing things and more swings sat off to the side of the property. There was also a basketball hoop at the end of the driveway.

Naomi's heart warmed. He was clearly comfortable being a dad.

As she parked in his driveway, she noticed a small face pressed against the front window. By the time she climbed out of the car with her dessert box, it was gone, but a moment later, Shane swung the door open wide.

Her first glimpse of the man always made her heart seize. No one had the right to be so attractive, with his broad shoulders, slim waist and handsome face.

Next to him stood Shane's son, a mini version of his father, right down to the way they both stood—weight on one leg, arms around each other—even if Shane's arm was around the boy's shoulders, and Brady's arm was slung around his dad's waist.

She swallowed. "Hello," she said, walking toward them. "You must be Brady. Your dad talks about you all the time."

Brady smiled, before eyeing the box.

"What's in there?"

Naomi shook her head. "Nothing you'd be interested in. I stopped at the Sweet Tooth Bakery and picked up doughnuts for dessert."

His eyes widened, and he looked up at Shane.

"Dad, I like doughnuts. Did you tell her I didn't?"

Shane bit his lip to keep from smiling. "Nope, I didn't say anything about doughnuts."

Brady turned back to Naomi. "I like doughnuts."

"You do?" She pretended to be shocked.

He nodded his head up and down so hard Naomi worried he'd give himself a headache.

"But do you like caramel chocolate chip doughnuts? Because those are my favorite."

Brady opened his mouth wide. "I *love* caramel chocolate chip doughnuts!"

Naomi smiled. "We like the same thing. How cool is that?"

The boy elbowed his dad. "She likes doughnuts, Dad."

Shane nodded. "I know."

Naomi wasn't sure what the significance of her liking doughnuts was, but she breathed a sigh of relief she'd passed the first test.

Brady frowned. "But did you get enough?"

She opened the box, and he peered inside, nodding his head. "That's good. Because otherwise we'd have to share."

"Well, if I had to share with anyone, I'd definitely pick you," she said. "But now, we can all have our own. And there's even an extra one to save for another day."

His eyes brightened. "Dad, can I have the extra doughnut? Please!"

Shane laughed. "How about we let Naomi inside, okay?"

They both ushered Naomi inside the house, Brady keeping his eyes trained on the box like it would disappear.

"You sure know how to please a six-year-old," Shane murmured as he led the way to the back of the house where the kitchen was.

Naomi barely had a chance to register what the house looked like, other than it gave off homey vibes with blues and beiges.

The kitchen, however, was huge and clearly meant to be the center of the home. She noted the stainless steel appliances were top-of-the-line, the cabinets a warm oak and the countertops designed in a beige granite with flecks of gold. Wooden stools were tucked under the counter of the center island, and a large oak table with six chairs sat in front of sliding doors leading outside to a large deck. The table was set for the three of them, and the scent of garlic and tomato made Naomi's stomach growl.

"The doughnuts will go great with the ice cream I picked up," Shane said. "I kind of focused on the main course."

She watched him drain pasta and toss it with meatballs and sauce, then pull garlic bread from the oven. A tossed salad already sat on the table.

"Can I help with anything?" she asked.

"Nope, we're all set," he answered. "Brady, can you get the napkins, please?"

The boy scrambled to grab three cloth napkins from the counter. He put them at each place and then climbed into his chair.

"Naomi, you can sit over there," he said, pointing to the seat opposite him. "My dad sits over here." He tapped his dad on the shoulder. "This can be Naomi's seat. You know, for the next time she comes over."

Her insides warmed at Shane's son taking to her so well.

"Thanks, Brady."

She sat down and remained quiet as they all served each other dinner.

"I'm so excited to have pasta and garlic bread," she said.

"With Passover coming up so soon, I need to load up on my carbs before I have to cut most of them out."

"Oh, that's right," Shane murmured. "It's almost Easter, and I remember the holidays usually take place near each other."

"I can't wait for Easter!" Brady gushed. "We have an egg hunt at my grandma's house with all the cousins, a huge dinner, and then I get an Easter basket at my mom's house."

"That sounds like so much fun," she said. "We do something similar to an egg hunt, but we search for matzah at the end of our seder, which is our special meal. In fact—" she leaned closer to the table "—we can't finish the meal until someone finds it."

"What happens to dessert?" Brady asked.

She shrugged. "We only get it if we find the matzah."

"So, if nobody finds it?"

She winked at Shane. "Then no one can leave the table."

"Ever?" Brady's eyes widened.

"Ever."

Brady looked at Shane with a serious expression. "Dad, we *have* to go to their seder. They need help, and I'm a great finder."

Ruffling his son's hair, Shane laughed. "That you are, kiddo." He turned to Naomi. "We've had more than one birthday or Christmas gift uncovered before the holiday."

"Wow, you sound like an expert."

Brady stuck his chest out. "That's me. I can find anything! I'm even helping my dad find a wife."

Naomi stifled a laugh as Shane turned beet red. Brady was adorable. As he launched into a spirited recitation of all the things he'd found, Naomi's heart filled with joy. Not only was he a great kid, but he was creative and personable and funny.

"Mom and Kevin have a really hard time hiding presents from me," he said. "One time, my mom asked me to get something out of the closet, only she forgot that's where she'd hidden a birthday present, and I came out with what she'd asked me to get…and a Nerf gun set." He grinned, the gap where his tooth had fallen out on full display.

"Oh my, your mom must have been sad to have spoiled the surprise."

"She was at first, but I gave her a big hug to make her feel better, and I didn't play with it until my birthday, even though I really, really wanted to."

She touched her chest. "That was so nice of you, Brady."

After dinner, Brady helped Shane clear the table while Naomi placed the doughnuts on a serving plate and helped get the ice cream ready.

A lot of whispering came from the kitchen, and she strained to hear.

"…make a great wife for you, Dad."

"Brady, that's enough."

She shook her head. That was what she got for snooping. There was no way Shane was going to take dating advice—or marriage advice—from a child.

They returned to the table, Brady's eyes once again focused on the plate of doughnuts. Shane was staring at them, too.

She laughed as she looked between Shane and his son.

"I'm not sure who's more excited about dessert. The two of you are practically drooling."

Brady, being a typical six-year-old boy, thought this was hilarious, and spent the next several minutes trying to wipe his dad's face. Naomi watched them interact, admiring the clear adoration the two of them had for each other.

This was the kind of family dinner she wanted. Whomever ended up with Shane was going to be one lucky woman.

They all dug into their treats.

"Naomi, you can provide dessert anytime," Shane said. "These doughnuts are amazing."

"Dad, you know, if Naomi was…you know…we could have doughnuts all the time."

Shane cleared his throat. "Give it a rest, Brady."

The boy wasn't very subtle, and Naomi decided to help Shane out. Mostly by ignoring Brady's interruption. "The bakery is one of my favorite places to shop. I just wish I could serve them for Passover."

Shane turned to her with interest. "What do you do about dessert if you can't eat bread?"

"We have special recipes we make, and a lot of them are quite good. Plus, Abuela Rosa Chocolates usually makes special Passover chocolate for us."

"I love Abuela's chocolate!" Brady cried.

"I'm starting to suspect you like anything sweet." Naomi smiled. "Just like me."

"You've got his number," Shane agreed.

"My whole family likes sweets, too. Especially my dad," Naomi told them. "My parents and all my aunts and uncles and cousins will be joining my grandmother for the seder this year, and I'm providing dessert."

She looked at the plate in the center of the table. There was one doughnut left.

"Brady, I'm going to leave the extra doughnut for you and your dad, okay?"

"Yeah!"

"What do you say, Brady?" Shane asked.

"Sorry. Thank you, Naomi. See, Dad, I told you she'd be perfect."

"You're welcome," she said, laughing. "And it's hard to remember manners when you're looking at a delicious doughnut."

"Yeah, Dad," Brady agreed.

Shane held up his hands in mock defeat. "As long as you're polite, that's all I want." He looked over at Naomi, his expression easy and happy. Clearly he was in his element, and she enjoyed seeing this side of him. She wasn't sure if he'd forgotten or not, but he didn't look like he was trying to impress her.

Which made him all the more appealing to her.

"How about we go into the family room and play a game?" Shane suggested. "Brady, why don't you go pick something out the three of us can play while Naomi and I straighten up in here."

With a nod, Brady bounced off his chair and ran into the other room.

"You don't actually have to help me clean up," Shane added when Brady was out of the room. "I just thought it would be nice to have a moment or two alone."

Naomi rose and began to bring over the empty dishes. "I don't mind helping," she said. "And your son is adorable."

"Thanks, he's a great kid. We really lucked out with him. And he really likes you. In fact," Shane said with a chuckle, "he thinks I should marry you."

Naomi laughed. "Yeah, I got that impression." She leaned against the counter as he loaded the dishwasher and tried not to notice the flex of his arm muscles. "But don't knock your skills. You make it sound like his behavior was up to chance. I think it has a lot to do with the type of parent you are."

He looked up at her, his heated gaze intense. The air around them crackled, and Naomi swallowed. After a moment, he ushered her out of the kitchen and into the family room. "Thank you."

"Dad, finally. Let's play Jenga."

Naomi stopped in the doorway of the family room, taking in the snapshot of the father-son duo.

A large stone fireplace took up one third of the facing wall, with floor-to-ceiling windows on either side of it. Navy sofas faced each other, with a low wooden and granite table in between. Brady had set up the Jenga game on the table, and knelt on the blue and beige rug, his back to the fireplace. Shane was in the process of starting the fire.

She entered the room, noticing the walnut bookcases and reading nook to her right and a piano with another seating area and bar to her left. The room was comfortable and family oriented, just like Shane.

"Do you know how to play, Naomi?" Brady asked.

"I do," she answered, walking over and taking a seat on one of the sofas. "My cousins and I used to play when we were younger. We still like to play together occasionally."

Once the fire was lit, Shane sat across from Naomi. "Ready?" he asked.

Brady was impatient, so the blocks he removed caused lots of wobbling. Shane was daring, and Naomi couldn't believe some of his maneuvers. She was more cautious with a steady hand. She laughed with them as they played, with Brady losing the first round and Naomi winning.

"Again!" Brady cried as he began restacking the tower.

Shane looked at Naomi, silently questioning if she wanted him to object.

"I'd love to play again," she said, touched at his concern for her.

The huge smile Brady gave warmed her heart, and for a moment, she could almost pretend she was a part of this family. Shane's pride in his son shone on his face, giving him a depth she hadn't noticed before. Brady brought out the fun-loving side of his dad. He was less controlled, less concerned about what anyone other than his son thought about him. More confident.

Naomi liked it.

Once again, she chose her bricks carefully, only this time, Shane won.

"Okay, bud, bedtime for you."

Brady stood up. "But Dad, we need a championship!"

Naomi paused in her cleanup of the bricks. "What kind?"

"You and Dad, to see who wins." He turned to Shane. "Please?"

Shane looked as though he was going to refuse. Naomi raised a brow in challenge.

"Fine. But then you're going to bed. No arguments, okay?"

"I promise!"

Brady's gleeful grin bled over to Naomi, and she hurried to collect the bricks. She'd never been particularly competitive, but this time, she wanted to win. Sitting across from Shane, she watched him put the last level on in the box, flip it over and stand the tower on the table. This was it. She focused on the bricks in front of her, testing and calculating each time it was her turn. Holding her breath, she pulled a brick. The tower wobbled but remained standing. Shane, using his usual daring strategy, pulled a brick she was sure would make the entire thing collapse. She gasped when it remained standing. This time, she tested and considered in frustration, as every brick she chose was firmly wedged. She groaned in frustration.

"You can do it, Naomi," Brady whispered.

She thought she heard Shane chuckle, but when she glanced at him, his face was a mask of innocence.

Finally, she chose the brick she thought had the best chance of keeping the tower intact.

She pulled, and the tower crashed.

"Whoop, I win!" Shane cried, before leaning over and shaking her hand. "Good game," he said.

"Dad!" Brady's voice was filled with exasperation.

"What?"

"You're supposed to let Naomi win. How else is she going to want to marry you?"

Oh boy, this kid had it bad. Naomi jumped in. "What? I don't want him to *let* me win."

Shane joined in. "That's not right, Brady."

"Why not?" the child asked as the three of them cleaned up the game.

Naomi's mind whirled. Brady was six years old. He couldn't really mean marry, could he? Her body went hot and cold. Meanwhile, why was she acting like a high schooler?

"Brady, I want to win on my own talent, not because your dad lets me," she explained.

"Exactly," Shane said. "If I let her win, it tells her I don't believe she can do it herself."

The six-year-old frowned, looked between the two of them and nodded his head.

"So, you still like him?" Brady asked Naomi.

"Of course," she said, shifting a little in her seat. "In fact, I'd like him less if he'd let me win."

At that, Brady gave a huge grin. "Good. Dad, you should beat her more often, then."

Rising from the sofa, Shane laughed. "Bedtime." He turned to Naomi. "Do you mind waiting down here for a minute? Since we played an extra game, we're not reading, so I won't be long."

"Not at all," she said. Her heart squeezed at the image of Shane reading Brady a bedtime story.

This man.

Brady ran over and hugged her waist. "Good night, Naomi."

She blinked, fighting the sudden tears that pricked her eyes. "Good night, Brady. It was great meeting you. I had a lot of fun with you."

"Me, too."

With a wave, he went upstairs with his dad, leaving Naomi alone.

"Sorry about that," Shane said to Naomi as he entered the family room once more. "I hope you didn't mind the wait."

She turned to him, the light of the fire making her skin glow. "Not at all. He's so good about bedtime."

Shane beamed. "He's a good kid all around. Honestly, no matter what we might have gotten wrong in our marriage, Lacey and I have really worked hard to get parenting Brady right."

"It shows. I had a lot of fun with him, too."

"I'm glad. So, you think I'll be able to find someone willing to take me and Brady on?"

A funny look crossed her face, intriguing Shane. She was so expressive. He'd never realized that about her. At first glance, she appeared so polished and professional, but the more time he spent with her, the easier it was for him to see behind that facade.

"I think anyone who wants kids would love to have Brady as a stepson," she said after a moment or two had passed.

He walked over to the bar and grabbed a bottle of wine and two glasses. Then he folded himself onto the same sofa she sat on and poured for both of them.

"Cheers," he said

Their glasses chimed as they touched, and they each took a sip of the red wine.

She placed hers back on the table and turned toward him.

"You have a spot of wine," he said, leaning forward and touching the corner of her mouth with his finger.

She blushed. Her rosy cheeks, warmed by the fire and reflected in the wineglass, painted a beautiful palette. Not surprisingly, her skin was warm to the touch.

If he were dating her, he'd lick the droplet of wine off his finger. But he wasn't, so he wiped it off with his thumb.

Why *wasn't* he dating her again?

She was beautiful, intelligent and loved kids. They got along well. And he was attracted to her.

She had a boyfriend.

Right.

And no matter what he might be tempted to do, he didn't cheat or help others to do so.

Instead, he stared at the fire.

The silence stretched between them, fragile like a spider's web. As if one word would break the trust and ease they'd established between them. Or maybe it was already destroyed since he'd touched her cheek.

He flexed his hand convulsively. He could still feel the imprint of her skin against the pad of his finger.

She cleared her throat.

Their gazes locked before she averted hers.

Whatever comfort she'd felt before seemed to have evaporated. It was up to him to get it back.

"How long have you been an image consultant?" he asked.

Satisfaction overtook him as she visibly relaxed. Clearly, talking about her work was the way to go.

"Officially? About five years," she said. "Unofficially, I think I've always been one."

"It's great when you can do something you love."

She nodded. "It rarely feels like work at this point. Unless I get an exceptionally stubborn client. But even then, I like the challenge."

"Have you ever dropped a client? Or had one you couldn't work with?"

She took another sip of wine, put her glass down again and sat back against the sofa. "Not many, but there have been one or two. They've tended to be higher profile clients, who were referred to me by their business managers but didn't really want to make any changes."

"I'd heard you've worked with celebrities, but I wasn't sure if that was a rumor."

She smiled but didn't comment. He liked that about her.

"How about you?" she asked. "Have you always wanted to work on the ranch, or did you ever dream of going away and doing something different?"

"I love this place," he said. Satisfaction made his chest expand. "My cousins and siblings and I grew up together, and despite our parents' friction, we've always gotten along. I wouldn't want to leave all this behind and go somewhere else. It's part of the reason why I want a big family. So that my kids can experience the same thing."

Naomi's expression turned wistful. "I've always loved celebrating holidays with my extended family. You're lucky to have grown up so close to yours."

"What holidays besides Passover do you celebrate to-gether?" he asked.

Naomi listed them, counting on her graceful fingers as she did so. "My mom hosts a big Rosh Hashanah dinner to celebrate the Jewish New Year, and my aunt has a break-the-fast dinner at the end of Yom Kippur. And my aunt on the other side of the family hosts a Hanukkah party."

Shane paused. "You have a breakfast dinner?"

He must have said something funny because Naomi started laughing.

"Sorry to laugh. We fast on Yom Kippur to atone for our sins. At sundown, we have a meal to break our fast."

Now he understood. He laughed as well. "Got it. That makes much more sense. At first I thought you meant breakfast for dinner, which is actually one of my favorite things, but then I was like, no, she didn't say that."

Naomi nodded. "I can totally understand why you'd think it."

She leaned against him for a moment, and suddenly, her proximity awakened the attraction that had been building. Naomi was a beautiful woman, and when she relaxed, there was something so vibrant and appealing about her. She practically transfixed him.

"I forget that not everyone knows about Jewish tradi-tions," she continued, oblivious to his desire.

He tried to focus on the conversation. "Your religion is important to you."

She nodded. "Very. It's all wrapped up in my family connection and my beliefs and who I am. Even though I'm not particularly observant, it still forms the foundation of who I am."

He admired someone who could be so honest about something like that. "I think, in a way, it's similar to my family connection," he said. "Family is everything to me, and although it's not the same, I think it's similar enough that I understand."

When she looked at him, without shying away from his gaze, something inside him came alive. They'd each bared part of their souls, talking about what really mattered, and while their foundations, as she called them, were different, they understood each other. That understanding was an aphrodisiac. An invisible connection tightened once again between them. The air around them grew charged. His heart pounded, and he focused on her lips. What would it be like to kiss her? One kiss. That was all he wanted. Just to remind him that they weren't right for each other.

Before he could stop himself, he drew her to him and took her mouth in his. Her lips were soft, and she tasted sweet, like the wine they shared. Passion exploded as their mouths opened and their tongues met, tentatively at first. She raised her arms and placed her hands on his shoulders. He wrapped his arms around her and explored her mouth, deeper, until he was consumed by her. She sighed, her tongue tousling with his. Raising his hand to the back of her neck, he twined his fingers through her hair, her silky strands wrapping around his hand.

She sighed again, pulling away, and reality returned. And with that came the realization that one kiss would never be enough for him. His body hummed with desire even as the voice in his head yelled at him and filled him with dismay.

He swallowed. "I'm sorry," he rasped. "I shouldn't have done that."

Her brown eyes were cloudy, and her breath came quickly.

"No, it's okay."

"It's not," he said, his tone belying his disappointment. "You're dating someone. I can't believe I let myself do that. I've never been one to cheat or be okay with others cheating."

She blinked a few times before blurting, "We broke up."

He stared at her, unsure if he heard her right or if it was some lust-filled fantasy of his that was still catching up with reality. "What?"

She closed her eyes before opening them once again. This time, her eyes were filled with pain. "He broke up with me six months ago." An odd look passed across her features before she continued. "I haven't said anything because…it took me a long time to get over him." Her gaze drifted away.

Sympathy welled. He understood her pain. He and Lacey, even though they hadn't been right for each other, still, the breakup hurt. Maybe that was why he felt a connection with Naomi. They'd both experienced a similar heartbreak. He waited her out, giving her space to collect herself.

"Plus—" she gave a half-hearted laugh "—it doesn't exactly speak well of me if I can't even keep my own relationship working."

"Seriously?" A lump formed in his throat. "You really think clients are going to find fault with you because your life isn't perfect?" He couldn't believe people would judge her for that. "I don't."

She gave him an odd look. Didn't she believe him?

"Well, I still don't want it getting around." She shook her head. "I didn't exactly mean to tell you, so I'd appreciate your discretion."

Something was off. He couldn't pinpoint what it was exactly. Maybe she just hadn't told him everything. He didn't blame her for that. They didn't have a relationship that went deep enough, despite his body telling him it wanted more.

His chest tightened. It wasn't just his body that wanted more from her. His mind did, too. He enjoyed their conversations, he loved watching her with his son, and he'd had fun with her whenever they were together.

"I won't say anything to anyone," he assured her. "But I still think you can go out on dates even if you're an image consultant. You're not immune to relationship troubles."

She held out her hand as if to stop him. "It's fine. I'm not in the market for a boyfriend, anyway." Color filled her cheeks. She was so darn beautiful when she blushed. But he couldn't possibly fall for the first woman he had good chemistry with. All the other women he'd dated had been perfect on paper, but not in reality. In their eyes, he was a cash cow. To find someone he truly could care for and be comfortable around, and who wanted him for who he was inside, was going to take time. A lot more time than what he'd spent with Naomi. He couldn't possibly know *now* that Naomi was right for him. And as a dad, he had to be especially careful when choosing a stepmom for his son. If he screwed this up, it would hurt Brady, too. Brady was dying for a stepmom, and he adored Naomi. But if Naomi wasn't the right woman for him, he'd disappoint his son.

He sighed in relief. "Well, as long as you're not upset at me for kissing you." He needed her to keep helping him.

She smiled, although it wasn't her typical one. It looked more forced. Was she upset about the kiss?

"No, I'm not," she said. "Don't worry."

The more time she spent with Shane and Brady, the more Naomi realized how badly she wanted a family. Possibilities she hadn't considered when she was younger and first learned she couldn't have children suddenly presented themselves, making her feel less like she was lacking and more like she had options. And, after spending this evening with the two of them, her desire deepened. This was what she wanted, and for the first time, she could see it in her future. She either wanted to adopt or marry someone like Shane, with a ready-made family.

In fact, her desire for a family was intertwining with her need for the handsome man she was helping.

Her neck tightened. Shane wasn't an option, no matter how amazing his kiss had been. She gripped her wineglass as she sat on the sofa, trying to keep her gaze off his lips, her mind off the sexy sounds he'd made as he took her mouth in his. Because if that kiss was to be believed, their chemistry was off the charts.

Her entire body hummed, her lips tingled and it took all her willpower not to touch them. Which left her little strength to resist leaning toward him and kissing him again. Because, oh, did she want to.

But she *couldn't*. She and Shane were completely wrong for each other. Despite her friendship with Poppy, she and Shane lived in different worlds. He was a wealthy Texas rancher, with a name that carried weight and family wealth. She was a Jewish woman who worked for every bit of success she'd had so far. And although both their lives revolved around family, those families were very different.

She'd put in so much time and effort with Andrew, and that had failed. After all the time they'd spent together, he'd cheated, wanting a biological family, something he couldn't have with her. There was no way she and Shane could just fall into each other's laps and work with such ease. Relationships took time and effort. She and Shane failed the first time. Whatever attraction she thought he felt for her could just be because she was there, in front of him. Like last time. She wasn't about to be his placeholder until the woman of his dreams walked by. Been there, done that.

Relationships required work. Talking and laughing with Shane was too easy. Too often she forgot she was supposed to be critiquing his dating skills.

Obviously, she was having rebound flutters. This was just her body's way of telling her it was ready to move on.

But not with Shane.

He was her client. So was his father. Talk about awkward. She didn't discuss her clients with people, but how was she supposed to pretend she wasn't seeing his father? That would require her to lie, and she hated lying. Plus, Garth would worry and probably drop her as his image consultant.

No, Shane was off-limits.

And even if she could get past all of the reasons they wouldn't work, she remembered how easily he'd walked away from her seven years ago. She'd thought they'd gotten along great. Clearly, she was lousy at reading him, so all of her assumptions tonight about what he felt for her had to be wrong.

She glanced at him as he sipped his wine, noting the relief on his face after telling him she wasn't available. See, right there. That wrinkle between his brows. No matter how much her finger itched to smooth it out, her brain knew that he was happy she was unavailable. She needed to listen to her brain more often. Her brain would keep her from getting hurt. Despite their chemistry, he wasn't interested in her.

Her heart pattered. *That was it.* He was relying too much on chemistry, on a woman who checked off all his boxes. He wasn't leaving any room for a relationship to progress naturally. She'd have to put that in his report. She looked around, trying to spot her bag with her phone.

"Do you remember where I left my purse?" she asked.

"You're leaving?" His eyes widened.

"Eventually," she said, "but I need my phone. I just thought of something and need to write it down, so I don't forget."

He placed his wineglass on the table and walked out of the room, his footsteps muffled on the carpet. He returned a moment later with her bag and handed it to her.

"Thanks." She pulled out her phone and jotted down what she wanted to add to his report on her notes app. Then she turned it off and dropped it back in her bag.

"I don't suppose you'll tell me what you wrote?" He tipped his chin toward her bag.

"If it's necessary, I'll put it in my report. But not everything I write down makes it in."

He swirled the remaining wine in his glass, staring into the ruby liquid, before swallowing it.

His Adam's apple bobbed up and down in his strong throat, and Naomi had to force herself to look away.

She tried not to fidget now that an awkwardness had risen up between them. Because he'd changed things from professional to personal and then back again. But she didn't know exactly where she fit. She tried to figure out a way to gracefully extricate herself from the situation.

Looking around, her gaze bounced off photos of Shane's family and Brady on the walls, equine books in the shelves, the gradation of blues and beige in the carpet. Anything to avoid looking at Shane.

She rubbed her palms on her thighs and finally looked back at him. "I should probably go," she said.

A myriad of emotions flickered across his gaze, but he

remained silent, only nodding in assent. Maybe she dreamed everything, she thought. Well, not the kiss. The kiss had happened, but she must have put a lot more emphasis on it than he did. This was another reason they shouldn't pursue a relationship. He didn't appear to want one with her, and if the desire wasn't equal, she didn't want to be a part of it.

Rising, she followed him back through the hallway to the front door.

"Thanks for coming tonight," Shane said.

"I loved meeting Brady."

His expression lightened. "I'm glad you two hit it off. He liked you as well. A lot."

"He's adorable." She swallowed. "Anyone would be lucky to be his stepmom."

He blinked, cleared his throat and opened the door. "Thank you," he stuttered.

As she walked outside in the cool night air, she thought to herself, *I kind of wish it could be me.*

Chapter Six

Shane buried his face in his hands. He'd blown it. He didn't know what happened, but once again, a great time with Naomi had turned awkward, and he didn't know what he was doing wrong. They all started out great. The conversation flowed, the laughter, the chemistry…and then somehow, everything fizzled at the end. He was madly attracted to her. So much so, it scared him. A future with her floated in the periphery of his vision, just out of his grasp, but egging him toward it. And he didn't know what to do about it.

Maybe it was Brady's constant suggestion he marry her. Anyone could feel uncomfortable about that. Six-year-olds didn't understand subtlety. He huffed. Brady's affection for Naomi shone in his bright eyes every time he looked at her, and he was dying for his dad to "get him a stepmom." Sure, Naomi had been a good sport, but it had probably spooked her.

He tapped his fingers on his knee. She'd just come off a long-term relationship. Was she comparing him to her ex? When he and Lacey had first divorced, he was gun-shy of any relationship, too, and wondered if all women were like his ex-wife. It was why he'd taken so long to dip his toe in the dating pool again. Perhaps she just needed more time to adjust to being single. Which meant he had to keep looking.

The following day, he went to Fortune's Gold Ranch to pick up a gift card for one of the ranch workers. Mabel had worked for them for ages and her birthday was coming up.

The weather was beautiful—a blue sky dotted with clouds, warmth wrapping around him like a blanket as he drank in the bluebonnets and other wildflowers starting to pop up in the open fields. He strolled along the path, trying to figure out what to do about Naomi as he walked toward the spa. He passed the café, filled with guests sitting outdoors, enjoying the weather and a bite to eat. He shook his head. Even though he knew better, they all looked carefree.

"Shane!"

At the sound of his sister's voice, he turned. Poppy pushed a stroller toward him.

"Hey, Poppy." When she reached him, he gave her a hug before kneeling down to peek at baby Joey, sleeping beneath the blanket.

"Gosh, he's adorable," Shane said. "I remember when Brady was that age."

Poppy smiled. "So do I. Listen, can you watch him for a few? There's a crisis at the spa I have to deal with."

He looked around and spotted an empty table at the café. "Sure, I'll just sit with him here. Hey, while you're there, can you pick me up a gift card for a massage?"

Poppy's eyes widened. "For your date?"

He scoffed. "I wish. No, it's for Mabel's birthday."

"Aw, that's sweet. You know, I have someone I want to fix you up with if you're interested."

Again? His sister had set him up many times since his divorce. Something about his needing to have fun since he'd rushed into marriage and fatherhood. But the idea didn't please him as much as it used to. It should. He was lonely and wanted to be in a relationship. The only way a relationship would happen was if he dated. However, the thought left a bitter taste in his mouth, since none of those dates had worked out. Did he really want to do this again?

Well, you hired Naomi for just this situation.

Dating someone his sister set him up with would be a great chance to try out the tips that Naomi's report would hopefully give him.

"Sure, go for it."

He took the stroller from Poppy and walked over to an empty table with an umbrella to shield Joey from the sun. Sitting down, he took the menu from the waitress and ordered a sweet tea. He waited, rocking the stroller a little and playing with his phone. But his mind remained on Naomi and how to avoid their awkwardness in the future.

"Shane?"

Letting go of the stroller, he twisted around in his seat. "Hey, Zach, how are you?" He rose and shook his hand.

Zach was a friend from a neighboring ranch. They'd gone to school together and occasionally met at the Emerald Saloon for a beer or a game of darts with friends.

"You up for another game soon?" Zach asked.

"So, I can beat your ass again? Of course," Shane said, grinning.

"I've been practicing. You're going down this time."

Shane grunted. "I'll believe it when I see it. Business good?"

The other man nodded. "Keeping an eye on the cattle. With the reports of sabotage, including at the Wellingtons', we're all on high alert. So far, no one's bothered us."

"Good to know. You're lucky."

Zach frowned. "Hey, is that your stroller?"

Shane whipped around in time to see a figure in black rushing away from the café with Joey's stroller.

With a yell, he and Zach raced after the person. Shane's heart was in his throat. His feet pounded the pavement in time to the roaring of blood in his ears, and they wove in and out of the passersby, ignoring their shouts of surprise. The only thing in his line of sight was the stroller. Just as they were gaining on them, the person let go of the stroller and disappeared into the tree line.

Shane grabbed the stroller, picking up Joey and cradling him against his chest as he tried to get his breathing back to normal. The warm body against his made his eyes prick as thoughts of what could have happened overwhelmed him.

"You okay?" Zach asked, hands braced on his knees. "And Joey?"

Shane's knees shook, and he squeezed the baby until he wiggled. With a shaky breath, he loosened his grip slightly, nodded to Zach and pressed kisses to the baby's head. As his adrenaline lessened, fear kicked in, and he closed his eyes, grateful he'd caught up to Joey in time.

When he was sure his legs would carry him, he and Zach made their way back to the café. Shane ignored everyone around him. Not letting go of the baby, he called the police, barking out his location and a quick summary of what happened. Then he called Poppy, dread making his chest ache.

"It's Shane. I need you back at the café. Someone tried to take Joey."

Poppy's gasp cut him to the core.

"Oh my God, is he okay? What happened? I'm on my way."

Her terror, her ragged voice, set off his fear once again, and he squeezed Joey against him, only letting up when the baby squeaked.

"He's fine, Pop-Tart, I've got him right here. He's safe. I promise he's safe." He'd never let him out of his sight again.

She hung up, and he repeated those words to himself, like a silent mantra, until her footsteps and cries of "Joey" made him turn around.

"Oh, baby, what happened?" She crooned to him as she took him from Shane, hugging him against his chest, as she pressed kisses to his face. Tears coursed down her cheeks.

After a moment, she leaned into Shane and the two of them held tight. Guilt at what he'd almost let happen overwhelmed him, until the police arrived.

For the next half hour, Shane and Zach sat with a police officer and described what they'd seen.

"Whoever took Joey was maybe five foot five," Shane said. "I'm six foot one, and the person was way shorter than I am, and pretty slight, too."

He looked at Zach. "Maybe it was a woman?"

Zach shrugged. "I didn't notice, but it could have been. It was hard to tell."

Shane pointed to where he'd lost track of the kidnapper, and showed the officers where he'd left the stroller. As some of them left in pursuit, and another one brought the stroller to the techs for fingerprint dusting, Shane returned to where Poppy and Joey sat with another officer.

"If it was a woman, do you think it was Joey's birth mother?" she asked, her face pale.

"Could be. Maybe she wants the baby back," Shane said under his breath. He texted Poppy's fiancé.

His sister closed her eyes and rocked Joey back and forth. "If it was her, I can understand wanting him, but she can't possibly think kidnapping is the way to go." Her voice wobbled, and Shane reached for her hand.

The police officer took notes, but gave a noncommittal answer. "We won't know until we catch whomever it was."

Leo arrived just then and raced over to Poppy. "Sweetheart, are you okay?"

He hugged his wife and baby, and looked at Shane. "Thank you."

Guilt made Shane's chest squeeze again. "You're *thanking* me? I almost lost your son."

Leo and Poppy shook their heads. "You got him back. That's all that matters."

Shane rested his head in his hands and fumed. Who the heck would try to kidnap a baby? It had to be the mother. But then another thought hit him. "Could it be whomever has been sabotaging the ranch?"

Poppy's face whitened. "Do you really think they'd go from cutting wire fences to stealing babies?" she asked, eyes wide.

Damn, he hadn't meant to scare her. He touched her arm. "I'm sorry. I was just thinking out loud."

The police officer took more notes. "It could also be someone looking for ransom, knowing the Fortunes have the wealth. Regardless of the motivation, we'll increase patrols around the ranch, and I'd suggest you all beef up your security."

When the police finished taking everyone's statements, they left. Shane said goodbye to Zach, and Leo drove Poppy and Joey home. As soon as he returned to his office, he called Garth and the rest of the family, who all promised to make sure more security measures were put in place.

But no amount of security was going to ease his guilt.

"Naomi, stop futzing with the matzah balls," her grandma said the next day, peering around her and swatting her hands. "You're going to make them sink like lead in everyone's stomachs."

Naomi yanked her hands out of the bowl and made fists with her hands. "Sorry. I was distracted." Oy, her grandmother was right. And no one liked lead-like matzah balls.

Bubbe nudged Naomi. "It's okay, but tell me what's wrong? You haven't seemed yourself since you arrived."

She washed her hands and dried them on the dish towel before sitting at the table, while her grandmother took over making the matzah balls.

"I don't know," she confessed. "I thought I did, but now I don't, and everything is confused in my head."

Bubbe speared her with one of her looks. "Obviously. But since I'm not a mind reader—please don't tell your mother that, she'll think I've lost my touch—you need to give me a hint of what's going on."

With a sigh, Naomi said, "Shane."

Her grandmother smiled. "If anyone was worth lead-like matzah balls, it would be him."

"Bubbe!"

"What?"

Naomi covered her ears. "I'm not having this conversation with you. Nope, we are not discussing matzah balls and Shane at the same time."

Her grandmother cackled. "Hey, you're going places I never intended."

"Ahhhh, no!"

Rising, Naomi paced the living room, trying to get the unwanted images out of her brain. She couldn't ignore the heat that pooled in her belly though.

"Relax, I'm finished," her grandmother said as she dropped the matzah balls into the pot of boiling seltzer. She turned down the heat, covered the pot and sat at the table. "Now spill."

Naomi joined her. "I think I'm falling for Shane. The

more time I spend with him, the more attracted to him I get. And I keep thinking that I would be perfect for him, even though I'm not, and even though things get awkward."

"Why don't you think you're perfect for him?"

"So many reasons. He's not Jewish. He's a Fortune. Every time things get…tense between us, he pulls away. And he apologizes and talks about the kind of woman he's looking for, which is clearly not me since I'm right in front of him, and last time—"

"Hold on," her grandmother interrupted. "Putting aside the religion and the name, you're not still focused on something that happened years ago after one week of maybe dating, are you? You're better than that, Naomi."

She frowned. "Better than what?"

"You are strong and smart and beautiful. You have way too much confidence to let one bad date with the man throw you completely off-kilter."

Her grandmother was fierce when she thought someone was being wronged. In this case, her ire was directed at her.

Naomi swallowed. Her grandmother was right.

"I think I'm conflating Shane and Andrew and tying everything together." She exhaled. "Andrew's change of heart threw me. He made me feel unworthy, and I'm just starting to get over that. And I guess I'm afraid to let myself fall for Shane, because what if he also decides he doesn't want me? He's already done it once."

"Then he's a schlemiel and not worth your time."

Naomi's eyes pricked with tears at her grandmother's steadfast support. "I love you, Bubbe."

"I love you, too. What is it about Shane that you like?"

"We have fun together. He's easy to talk to, charming, and he wants a family, as do I."

Her grandmother nodded. "You two have a lot in common. Have you talked about the differences in religion? Or your concerns about his family name?"

Naomi shook her head.

"Have you asked him how he feels about you?"

"No," she admitted.

"If you were your client, what advice would you give yourself?"

Naomi laughed and picked imaginary lint from her jeans. "To communicate."

Her grandmother put her hand on her arm and squeezed. "So, maybe you should listen to yourself. And maybe you *do* need some lead-like matzah balls."

Two hours later, Naomi was still cringing over her conversation with her grandmother. With Passover fast approaching, there was no way she was going to be able to bury the image enough in the deep recesses of her brain to be able to look at matzah ball soup, never mind eat it.

She shivered as she stepped outside the apartment, and it had nothing to do with the temperature. No, it was beautiful outside. Blue sky, light breeze, the scent of spring in the air. She couldn't believe her grandmother had not only joked about balls, but somehow turned it into a lesson for her. If she wasn't afraid the woman would scar kids for life, she'd recommend her as a Hebrew school teacher.

That image was enough to make her laugh.

Releasing the tension enabled her to consider what her bubbe had been trying to teach her, minus the matzah balls.

Until she'd verbalized her fears to her grandmother, she hadn't fully realized how much Andrew had hurt her by changing his mind and cheating on her. But he had. Even months later, she still felt nauseated when she thought about what he'd done.

She stopped dead on the sidewalk. That was it. What *he'd* done. Not her. Sure, every relationship took two people, and there was rarely a time when both parties weren't somewhat to blame, but he was the one who'd cheated on her. She deserved better, and the only way she was going to find better was to look for it. Or at least take advantage of opportunities that presented themselves.

Shane was an opportunity.

There was no guarantee that the two of them would work out, but she'd be a fool not to try. She had to learn to trust again. All current indications pointed to them getting along well—mutual attraction, mutual enjoyment and mutual goals.

So why not? Why not open herself up to the possibility that she and Shane should give a relationship a try?

Maybe the withdrawals she'd sensed were because he was a client. If that was the case, she had to talk to him and tell him that being a client didn't necessarily mean they couldn't be together. Especially since the reason he was a client was he wanted to find a life partner.

Bottom line? Nothing would happen unless she faced her fears, learned to trust and had a conversation with him.

Newly resolved to give him a chance and address the issue, she turned around and almost ran smack into Garth and Shelley.

"Whoa, there," Garth boomed, smiling as he grabbed her arms to keep her on her feet. "I didn't mean to run you over," he said. "Please forgive me."

He stepped back and put his arm, once again, around his wife's shoulders. "Naomi, you know Shelley, right?"

"Of course. It's nice to see you both again. I was just leaving my grandmother."

She knew better than to tell Shelley her husband was a

client, but she was stunned by how well Garth had transformed himself. No longer the brusque, curt man who probably would have blamed *her* for running into *him*, he was chivalrous and friendly.

Judging by the content look on Shelley's face, she'd noticed the improvements, too.

"Oh, that's nice," the older woman said. She looked up at the building. "It's a lovely place, and so nice that you're able to visit her easily."

Naomi nodded. "Every day. Especially now that we're getting ready for Passover."

Shelley smiled. "That's right, it's coming up soon, isn't it?"

"It is. The whole family is coming in to celebrate."

"We'll be having everyone for an egg hunt and Easter dinner as well," Shelley said. "I just love big family get-togethers, don't you?"

"Yes, they're a lot of fun."

"Shelley, don't you think she and Shane would be great together?" Garth said.

Naomi's eyes widened.

He turned to her. "I was telling Shelley just the other day how easily I could see the two of you together."

"Garth, honey, don't embarrass the woman."

Naomi's face was already warm. Now that they'd noticed, she wanted to drop through the sidewalk to the Earth's core. Not that it would be any warmer there, but at least she could melt away in peace.

"Gosh, I'm sorry, Naomi," Garth said. "Especially since you've already got a boyfriend, and Poppy is trying to set up Shane with someone."

Naomi's stomach dropped. Poppy was setting him up? With whom? When? The news shouldn't have surprised her, since the whole reason he was meeting with her was to improve his dating skills, but now that she'd acknowledged her feelings for him, it was like a gut punch. Still, she tried to hide her reaction.

"That's okay, really," she said, trying her best to make her voice firm.

"It's all in the timing," Shelley said. "Speaking of which, we've got to get going. So nice to see you, Naomi."

"Nice seeing you both as well," she murmured.

She left, more determined than ever to talk to Shane and tell him her feelings.

Chapter Seven

Bright and early the next morning, Shane called Naomi on his way to the office. His heart quickened when she answered, her voice cheerful and bright.

"Hey, Shane, I was just thinking about you. I wanted to talk to you."

He couldn't help the grin that spread across his face. "Well, that's the nicest thing I've heard all day."

She laughed. "It's eight thirty in the morning. How much competition could I possibly have?"

"You'd be surprised how many people want to talk to me. But you're by far the best."

"Aw, thank you."

Her warmth wrapped around him. "Anyway, the reason I called was to thank you for all your help and to ask if you had the latest report for me. Poppy set me up on a date with her friend Chloe. I'm seeing her tonight, and I want to make sure I cover all the areas you've suggested for improvement."

"Oh."

Her voice was decidedly less cheerful now. Maybe since they were talking work, she was trying to sound more professional. She was a successful image consultant. Of course, she would have perfected her own image.

She cleared her throat and continued. "Of course. I can send it over right now."

Shane opened his email inbox and sure enough, Naomi's message came in.

"Thank you. According to my sister, Chloe checks off all my boxes and will make a great stepmom. I'm actually looking forward to the date."

He was. He tapped his fingers on his desk. After reminding himself that dating was the whole reason he'd hired Naomi in the first place, and going over all the pointers she'd given him so far, he'd shed his reluctance. All he had to do was scan this latest report. Then dinner out would be great. He'd picked the perfect place for a first date—Cucina. The Italian restaurant was romantic, perfect for a date.

"That's great. I hope it works out for you."

She was quiet, and his usual awkwardness stretched across the line. He struggled to fix things.

"How are you?" he asked. "Brady didn't stop talking about you all morning."

Naomi's laugh filled him with relief. "That makes me so happy, although I apologize for you having to listen to it."

"Trust me, you're a much better subject of conversation than the frogs he catches by the creek."

She grunted. "Great, I'm better than frogs. Good to know."

He kicked himself. Talk about being an idiot. "Oh damn, I'm sorry. I didn't mean—"

"I'm teasing you," she said. "It's fine. But unless there's something else, I need to go. I've got a meeting in a few minutes."

Relief mingled with disappointment. "I'll let you go,

then. But wait, wasn't there something you wanted to ask me?"

"Hmm? Oh, no, never mind. As long as you've got my latest report, it's fine."

He frowned. Again, her voice had changed. "Well, one of these days I'll stop putting my foot in my mouth. Hopefully, before tonight's date."

"Bye, Shane."

He spent the rest of the day at the ranch offices, pouring over the mounds of paperwork his secretary had left for him, and fielding phone calls from the stable manager about security. Between the fence sabotage and Joey's almost kidnapping, everyone was taking every precaution. Especially him. He triple-checked everything, vowing never to put Joey at risk again.

He called his sister that evening on his way to Cucina, guilt over his role in Joey almost being kidnapped still eating at him.

"Hey, Pop-Tart, you and Joey okay?"

"We're fine, Shane. Really."

The pressure in his chest eased. "Good."

"You all set for the date?" Poppy asked.

"As I'll ever be," he said. "Any last-minute advice?"

"Just be yourself."

He shook his head. He'd worked so hard to change himself, he wasn't sure how to follow Poppy's advice. His palms were clammy, and he gripped the steering wheel a little harder as he turned into the parking lot of the Emerald Ridge Hotel, where Cucina was located. The fancy hotel, located in the center of town, attracted an elite clientele. Although he could afford the prices, he preferred a more casual vibe that was warm and welcoming. However, Cucina's chef was fantastic, and he loved their Italian food.

After leaving his truck and his keys with the valet, he entered the lobby, taking a quick glance at his reflection in the glass doors. Jeans, white button-down shirt, deep gray blazer and his gray cowboy hat. He hoped Chloe was happy with his appearance. Taking a deep breath, he passed the reservation desk, his boots echoing on the marble floors, and turned toward the sitting area in front of the restaurant. He was early, but Chloe was already there.

She stood to greet him, her blond hair flowing around her shoulders, a bright smile on her face and a black sleeveless dress emphasizing her curves.

His nerves disappeared.

"Hi, Chloe? I'm Shane."

"Good to meet you," she said. "Poppy told me you were easy on the eyes, but I don't think she did you justice."

She was direct, he'd give her that. He swallowed. "My sister clearly believes in understatement." He gave her an appreciative look before placing his hand at her lower back. "Shall we?"

She looked up at him sideways, leaned into him a little, before saying, "Yes," and walking with him into the restaurant.

Make that very direct.

The restaurant was slightly industrial-looking, with large copper pendulum lights hanging from the ceiling, white walls and a huge copper and granite island in the center where the cooking took place. Floor-to-ceiling windows on two sides overlooked the courtyard of the hotel. The hostess led them to a corner table, with a white linen tablecloth and candles flickering softly. Above them, huge glass chandeliers sparkled.

They chatted about the restaurant and what food they were in the mood for. Once the waiter took their order and the sommelier brought their wine, Shane leaned forward, eager to get to know the woman sitting across from him.

"Other than telling me that you're great, Poppy didn't give me much detail about you," he said. "Tell me the most important thing I should know about you."

Chloe blinked. "I'm a huge castle fan."

Out of all the things she could have said, he hadn't expected her to say that.

"*Castle*? Like the TV show?"

She laughed. It was a perfectly fine laugh, but it didn't make his insides hum.

"No, like an actual castle. You know, the kind royalty lived in at one time. Or actually, still do."

His confusion cleared. "Oh, I get it. Have you visited any?"

She nodded. "I try to travel at least once a year. I've been all over Italy—they have some beautiful ones."

For the next several minutes, she regaled him with stories from her trips, even showing him photos of some of her favorite castles.

Shane nodded along, enjoying how animated she became when talking. "Your photos are gorgeous," he said.

"Thanks. My dream, of course, is to go to Transylvania. Their castles are stunning."

Transylvania? "Wow, that sounds like an amazing place."

She relayed her ideal itinerary. "What about you?" she asked. "Where do you want to travel?"

He hadn't really thought about it, to be honest. He loved Emerald Ridge, his proximity to his family and the Texas landscape. It fed his soul. Then, of course, there was Brady.

"Well, as a single dad of a six-year-old, my options are a little limited at the moment."

Chloe's face creased in sympathy. "Oh, does your ex give you a hard time about taking your son on vacation?"

"No, actually, she's great. We're very communicative, and I'm sure if I asked, she'd have no problem with my taking him somewhere. But he's young, and in school, and energetic. I think overseas travel is a little beyond him right now."

She nodded in understanding. "Of course. Besides, Europe is so much more fun without kids."

The waiter interrupted with their food, and Shane was thankful for the break. His stomach tightened at her eagerness to think of travel without kids. Sure, they were adults, and alone time was important, but his time with his son was limited enough as it was. He wanted family vacations filled with laughter and kid activities.

"I'm sure it can be," he said. "But I suspect national parks and amusement parks are going to be more my speed for a while."

While she didn't look appalled, her eagerness dimmed a little. Mentally, he shrugged. When you had a family, sacrifices had to be made.

She began to eat, asking about his job and showing interest in his responses. She was a financial planner, and they talked about the business side of the ranch for a while. But the entire time they spoke, Shane noticed how little she ate.

"Do you want to send that back for something else?" He pointed to her saffron scallops with his knife.

She shook her head. "It's delicious. It's just very rich, so I can't eat all of it. How is your beef fillet?"

"Excellent."

The rest of their dinner passed uneventfully. As did the end of their date. It was clear neither of them felt any spark.

"I enjoyed meeting you," he said, once they were back in the lobby, coats on, ready to leave.

She smiled. "Thank you for a lovely evening."

He hated this part of the date, not knowing quite how to say goodbye. Especially when he wasn't interested in a second date.

He walked her to the valet stand, and they chatted while waiting for her car. When the valet appeared with her Mustang, he helped her into it, kissing her hand before shutting the car door for her.

She rolled down the window, and he leaned in. "Drive safe," he said and watched her pull away.

He texted Poppy as he waited for his truck to be pulled round.

Thanks for the setup.

How'd it go?

Fine.

And it was. There was absolutely nothing wrong with Chloe or their date. But he wanted more than fine. There was no spark, and no desire to see her again. After all his training with Naomi, why wasn't this date better? Chloe was intelligent, a good conversationalist and pretty. Something was missing, though, and for the life of him, he couldn't figure out what.

"I think I need to stop dating for a while," Shane said to Naomi the next morning on the phone.

Her heart fluttered, which was weird. From the sound of it, things hadn't gone as well as Shane had hoped on his date last night. Which should mean that she hadn't done her job well enough. She should be concerned that she hadn't given him enough pointers. Or that he'd decide to look somewhere else for advice. So why did the thought of Shane off the market make her smile?

"What happened?" she asked softly.

"I have no idea," he said. His exasperation flowed through the phone. She could imagine him jamming his fingers through his hair. "We ate, we talked, but something was off, and I don't know what in the hell I did wrong."

She leaned against the counter in the little kitchenette in her office, cradling her cup of coffee in one hand, a handful of Lucky Charms in the other.

"Maybe you're not doing anything wrong," she mused, crunching the sugary sweetness.

"How is that possible? I've been on more dates in the last year than I can remember. I have to be doing *something* wrong."

Naomi thought about the "dates" she'd been on with him. "I don't think you are. Look at the report I sent you. Sure, there are little things you can improve on, but nothing you're doing or not doing screams bad date. Maybe it's them."

"All of them?" His voice rose with disbelief. "The only thing 'wrong' with Chloe, and it could have been my imagination, was we didn't jibe when it came to vacations. But that shouldn't be enough of a reason for the entire date to feel off. No, I think I need more practice with you."

She shouldn't feel the joy that warmed her at the thought of spending more time with him.

But she did.

"Okay, we can go on more dates," she said, trying to

keep the excitement out of her voice. "When are you available?"

"Let me check my calendar…"

Naomi sipped her coffee as she listened to him mutter to himself. There was something adorable about a frustrated Shane. Maybe this was the side he should show to potential dates. Dread filled her. On second thought, maybe not.

"Would you believe I'm booked from now until the weekend?"

She walked over to her desk and scanned her work plan. "That's okay, I'm busy this week, too. Why don't we plan for Saturday night?"

"Hey, do you like line dancing?"

Images of hora dancing at her cousins' weddings filled her mind. Somehow, she didn't think that was what he meant.

"I've never done it, but I'm happy to give it a try," she said.

"Great, the Cowpoke Brewery hosts line dancing every other Saturday night, and this Saturday is one of those nights. Want to go?"

She looked down at her feet in very expensive heels. Their elegance belied the fact that she had two left feet. Actually, left feet would probably be an improvement. She was a total klutz when it came to dancing. In fact, Andrew had lamented over it. One time and he'd never wanted to go with her again. Would Shane mind?

"I have to warn you I'm a terrible dancer," she told him.

He scoffed. "You can't possibly be worse than Poppy."

Naomi laughed. "I feel like terrible dancers have to stick together. Besides, I don't want to shame your sister."

He raised an eyebrow. "Oh, you can shame her all you want. I do it."

"Yes, but not when she's not here to defend herself."

He laughed. "True. However, I'm not sure there's anything to defend. Regardless, line dancing is easy. They tell you what to do and you copy everyone else. Trust me, you'll do great."

She didn't have nearly his confidence and took another scoop of Lucky Charms in the hopes it might help.

"Like I said, I'm willing to try."

"Great, I'll pick you up Saturday at seven. They serve a buffet, too. See you then."

Suddenly, her weekend plans were looking up. And maybe, if they had a good time, and her lack of dancing skills didn't scare him away, she could talk to him about dating for real.

Humming to herself, she dialed Garth's number.

"Hi, it's Naomi. How are your plans for the job fair coming along? Have you figured out a date yet?"

His voice, similar to Shane's, echoed through the phone. "I just talked to Steve at the high school. Great guy. They're planning to hold it the first week in May."

Naomi added it to her calendar. "That's awesome. Are you good with things or do you need help?"

Garth's deep laugh echoed in Naomi's ear. "Darlin', I've been forging connections with local businesses since before you were born. I've got it under control. But I appreciate all your help, and I'll keep you updated."

Naomi smiled. "Perfect. I'm so glad this is coming together. And the mentorship program?"

"I'm talking to my contacts about that as well. Don't worry, I've taken your suggestions seriously. You're already helping me more than you know."

Naomi's chest lightened at the praise. "Thank you, I appreciate hearing that. And I noticed you and Shelley seemed at ease with each other the other day."

He cleared his throat. "Shelley and I…"

His voice dropped off, and Naomi assumed he was distracted by business. But when he spoke again, embarrassment tinged his voice, making him sound younger.

"…we haven't been this close in a good long while. You saved my marriage."

Her eyes filled. "I'm so glad, Garth. But you're the one doing the work."

"Well, I can't thank you enough," he said, back to the brisk Garth she knew. "If you ever need anything, you come to me, hear?"

"I will, thank you."

She hung up, wondering if there was any way he could help her with his son.

Ha. Not likely.

Shane looked up from his desk in the Fortunes' ranch offices as his brother Rafe barged in and dropped a stack of papers on his desk.

"Hello to you, too," he said, frowning. "Since when don't you knock? Or at least ask if I'm busy?"

"Are you?" Rafe asked.

"That's not the point," Shane huffed.

"Then I don't see the problem." He turned toward the door, whistling as he went.

"Wait, what did you give me?"

"They're your share of the Gift of Fortune potential recipients. Poppy's got a stack as well. Look through them and star anyone you think might be good."

Shane shook his head as his brother disappeared, his whistle echoing down the hall. The man had been through hell and back, and while Shane was happy to see him in a better place, he'd be happier if his brother worked on his manners.

Maybe he should recommend Naomi's services.

He huffed and picked up the stack, riffling through it. One more thing to add to his to-do list this week. Great. And then he stopped himself. No, this was a good thing, a goodwill initiative. He and his siblings and cousins were privileged enough to lead a life without want of almost anything. This was their way of giving back. They opened up applications to people who needed a place to stay while they healed emotionally from something in their lives. The siblings and cousins got together and chose the most deserving of the applicants and awarded them a free stay at the Fortune's Gold Guest Ranch & Spa. His cousin Drake had come up with the plan. Rafe had even fallen for one of the recipients, Heidi Markham, which helped to explain his good mood.

It was a meaningful way to give back to others, and if it caused him a little extra work sometimes, it was totally worth it.

He skimmed some of the entries before forcing himself to get back to his original task. While the initiative was important, he couldn't focus on it to the exclusion of everything else. Especially with the security of the ranch—and Joey—at stake.

But throughout the week, in spare moments of time, he continued to read through the entries. He carried the stack with him wherever he went. In the stables, he pictured potential nominees riding horses. When he met with Poppy over at the spa, he imagined them getting massages and steam baths. Even at home, he envisioned recipients having the chance to relax for the first time in ages.

One applicant in particular stuck with him, a divorced father of four. It was the second entry he'd read, but each time he reviewed the stack, he returned to this guy's story. Nominated by a friend, the father was shell-shocked by his life blowing up unexpectedly. His divorce affected every aspect of his life, but especially his relationship with his children. The friend talked about how time at the dude ranch would be a great way for the father to reconnect, and maybe even find the courage to date again or fall in love.

Courage.

That was what stuck with Shane all throughout the week, and even now, as he entered the stables. The smell of hay, manure and horse greeted him. Some of the horses whickered while others stomped their feet in their hay-strewn stalls.

There were a lot of similarities between him and the divorced dad. Maybe that's why he couldn't get the application out of his head. Their lives had both fallen apart, even though his relationship with his ex was on friendly terms. Any ending was awful, though, and he'd worked hard to get to where he was today. The biggest difference between him and the other guy was his willingness to date. He was actively looking for love, but maybe looking wasn't the problem. He'd gone on lots of dates. Poppy and his brothers frequently offered to set him up with women they knew. But none of the dates were successful. His siblings thought he was looking to be too serious too fast. They thought he needed to loosen up and have fun.

What if they were wrong?

Maybe his problem had to do with courage.

Or lack of it.

At night, when he was alone with his thoughts, the idea of falling in love with someone and really letting down his guard scared the crap out of him. Maybe his failure at finding someone he wanted to date wasn't about what he *was* doing, but what he *wasn't*.

Maybe he wasn't letting his guard down enough to allow love to flourish.

He scoffed, the sudden noise spooking one of the horses he was petting. "Sorry, girl," he whispered.

His family would laugh at him for... Well, maybe they wouldn't laugh. Rafe had found love. So had Poppy. Even his parents' marriage looked like it was improving. His mother's eyes had lost that pinched look, and his father? Well, he was kinder than normal.

Maybe the only one not in touch with their feelings was Shane himself.

He'd have to talk to Naomi and get her opinion.

Just thinking about her now made his day brighter. She'd tried to help him improve his image. But lately, when he'd complained that it wasn't working, she hadn't suggested he change what he was doing. She'd said to consider the problem might not be him.

What if they were both wrong? What if it really was that he wasn't brave enough to let down all his barriers?

And what if Naomi was the right woman for him?

He staggered, leaning against the stable door to regain his balance. Naomi? Where had *that* thought come from? Sure, their practice dates had gone well, until something would happen to make things awkward.

Wasn't that a sign that they weren't right for one another?

But then again...he didn't know why things had gone south because he'd never been brave enough to ask.

So what if the next time they encountered a patch of awkwardness—since they'd had several in the past, it stood to reason it'd happen again—he stopped and asked? Maybe they could work through whatever held them back.

He scoffed. It shouldn't have taken him this long to ask himself this question. He was an adult; communication was supposed to be his go-to, not his last resort.

In the lead-up to seeing Naomi on Saturday, he wavered between excitement and embarrassment. He even tried on his jeans ahead of time to make sure he liked the fit.

If his brothers knew, they'd never stop teasing him. And his sister? Poppy would never let him live it down. Oh no, no one was going to ever know how much care he put into his—he scrunched his face in distaste—*outfit*.

When Saturday night finally arrived and it was time for him to pick up Naomi, he hopped into his truck and blasted some country music, just to let off steam and remind himself he wasn't the kind of guy to spend hours in front of the mirror. By the time he arrived at Naomi's, he felt more centered.

He met her at her door and helped her into his truck before jogging around and climbing in on his side.

Glancing to his right, he smiled at her. "You look great."

She was wearing a floral minidress and cowboy boots, and she looked gorgeous.

"Thanks." She looked down at herself and over at him. "I figured I should dress the part. You look good, too."

Her compliment pleased him way too much, and he focused on driving the short distance to the Cowpoke Brewery where the line dancing was held, rather than the heat racing up his neck. Boasting the best beer in the region, the owners took advantage of the tourists who flocked to the springs and made their brewery an attraction. In addition to tours and tastings at the actual brewery, they ran a thriving brews-and-brats bar and an event space in the back, where they hosted lots of activities. Tonight's event, as it was every week, was a favorite of locals and tourists alike.

Shane and Naomi entered the cacophonous bar and headed into the event space behind it. The room resembled a barn, with rough wood walls and a plank floor. From the ceiling, iron chandeliers hung evenly spaced, and twinkle lights were suspended from them, adding a festive well-lit air to the room. On one end, a raised platform held a microphone and several chairs for the band. At the other, appetizers of all kinds sat on buffet tables covered in burlap. Around the perimeter of the room, tables and chairs accommodated people who wanted to break for snacks or drinks.

Shane led Naomi to the buffet tables. "What would you like to start with?"

She made her choices, and he filled two plates with finger foods, depositing them, and Naomi, at a nearby table.

"I'll grab drinks from the bar," he said.

Naomi nodded. "Beer will be fine for me."

He left her at the table while he hurried back into the bar. Exhilaration raced up and down his spine. Nodding at some of his acquaintances, he asked the bartender for two IPAs and brought them back to the table.

"How often do you line dance?" Naomi asked.

"My mom loves it, and every year on her birthday, or close to it, she forces the rest of us to go with her."

He leaned toward her, trying not to laugh. "Don't tell her, but I actually kind of enjoy it."

"I'd hope so. Otherwise, I might wonder why I'm here. Especially since I don't dance."

Shaking his head, he dug into the queso dip. "I don't get it," he said. "You're so graceful. How do you *not* dance?"

She shrugged, taking a sip of her beer. "I was always the kid playing outside in the dirt."

His eyes widened. "You're kidding me. You?"

He allowed himself to stare at her entire body, taking in how her cowboy boots showed off her shapely calves, and how the sweetheart neckline of her dress emphasized her delicate collarbones. He swallowed.

"You don't look like the rough-and-tumble type."

"Looks can be deceiving," she said, brown eyes sparkling.

And once again, he was smacked in the face with something that sounded profound but shouldn't be.

Looks can be deceiving.

The women he'd tried dating had looked perfect to him. It was why he'd gone out with them in the first place. And each one had been disappointing.

Naomi gave off this untouchable vibe, yet she was down-to-earth and warm.

Why did it feel like he was going about his entire life the wrong way?

"Do you not agree?" she asked.

Before he had a chance to answer, the line dance caller announced it was time to get started.

Naomi stood next to Shane, biting her lip. "I'm going to make a fool of myself," she whispered.

Part of him wanted to give her a hug of reassurance. Another part of him wanted to pull her lip from her teeth... with his own mouth. The space between them ignited with desire. His pulse raced, and he took a few steps away from her to clear his head.

"Line up behind the person in front of you," he said, pointing to a woman dressed in jeans and a rhinestone vest. "The caller will tell you what to do. If you're not sure, just do what everyone else is doing. Trust me, it's easy."

She shook her head. "Sure it is."

But the music started, the caller yelled out the steps and

Shane, along with everyone else, started dancing. When he turned toward Naomi, he noticed how she was able to follow the steps, too.

Her face was bright with delight, and she winked at him as she spun around. Clearly, her innate grace came in handy.

Now that he knew she could do it, and would therefore have a good time, he relaxed. The stamping feet, the beat of the music and the aerobic activity lifted his mood. Naomi's smile and clear enjoyment made him love what they were doing even more. Each time they spun close to each other, the heat between them intensified.

And admiring her body as her dress floated around her was an added bonus.

A bonus he hadn't expected.

But the truth was, he'd thought about her all week. Her smile and bright eyes filled him with warmth. He admired her spirit of adventure, making his own heart race. And every time they were close to each other, sparks flew.

By the time the caller signaled a break, he was energized and ready for a drink.

And brave enough to tell her how he felt.

"Have you ever wondered if you were chasing the wrong path?" he began as they each nursed their drinks and munched on stuffed jalapeño poppers.

Naomi rested her chin in her hand. "Yes, often. Usually, it's when I'm presented with a difficult client, either one whose problem is tricky or who won't listen to any of my advice. Why? Are you having problems on the ranch?"

"No, well, yes, but I wasn't actually talking about business."

Her gaze focused on him, and she leaned forward. "Shane, I promise, you're going to find someone."

She didn't understand.

"Actually, I think I already have."

Right before she masked all expression, he thought he caught a glimpse of disappointment. He wasn't positive, but he hoped it meant he was on the right track.

"That's wonderful." Her tone was measured, and her knuckles whitened as she gripped her beer. "Tell me about her. How'd you find her? Is it the woman your sister set you up with? Or someone else?"

It was time for him to take a leap, one where he put himself at risk. But the best results usually came from the most precarious options.

Or so he hoped.

"She's beautiful." He studied Naomi's clear skin, luscious brown hair and velvety brown eyes. "She's elegant and smart and always knows what to do, but she's also got a hidden side—slightly wilder, less sure of herself, and totally adorable."

Naomi swallowed, her gaze darting to the side before returning to him. "She sounds…perfect for you."

"I think she might be. I've known her for a long time. In fact, she's been right in front of me all along, I was just too afraid to make my move."

Her mouth parted. "Really?" Her voice was huskier than usual.

Had she figured it out yet?

He nodded.

"When are you going to make your move?"

"Right now." He studied her as realization dawned.

Her eyes widened, and she licked her lips. Her cheeks reddened, giving her skin a rosy glow.

His chest tightened. He wanted *her*. Not someone else. And he was taking a leap here, that she'd want him back.

The longer she took to respond, though, the louder his heart pounded in his ears.

"She's here?"

Her question threw him for a moment, until her eyes sparkled.

"She is. Right across from me."

Her mouth trembled, and she covered it with her hand. "Is she?"

Shane nodded.

"How'd you figure it out?"

He reached for her hand. Her skin was soft, her fingers supple. She gripped his back, and once again, her strength surprised him.

He needed to remember there was more to her than met the eye.

"Well, it took me a lot longer than it should have." He ran his thumb over her knuckles. "I'm a little embarrassed, actually."

"The important thing is that you *did* figure it out," she said.

"What about you?" he asked. "How long did it take you?"

"Entirely too long as well."

"Guess we both have to work on that."

She nodded. "So does this mean you're firing me?"

He threw his head back and laughed. "Firing seems a little strong. Maybe furloughing?"

"So, we can see how it goes." She stared at their entwined hands.

"Make sure we're doing it right." He leaned toward the middle of the table.

"Correct any mistakes as they happen." She gazed at his mouth, their faces barely an inch apart.

"Sounds good." He caressed her cheek before placing a soft kiss on her lips.

"Feels good, too," she whispered when he pulled away.

"Does this mean you're ready to try us?"

She nodded. "It's good to take risks and try new things."

Chapter Eight

Naomi awoke the next morning, her head filled with dreams of Shane. She couldn't remember the details, only that he'd been with her, and she'd been happy, pillowed by joy and contentment.

As for their date last night, she remembered everything. "Achy Breaky Heart" had been her favorite dance, the tempo and steps easier for her two left feet to comprehend. Shane's jeans had been indigo and had sculpted his butt, making her mouth water. He'd smelled like pine and mint, and when they'd leaned across the table to kiss, his scent had made her heady with desire.

And his kiss? Good lord, that man could kiss.

They'd kissed in the past, but honestly, she'd been so overcome by the results of their first, horrible date, she'd had barely any recollection of his kiss.

This time around though? Whoa.

Super short, it had been tender and soft, a promise of what was to come. And afterward when he'd taken her home?

Well, *that* kiss had been longer, deeper, sexier. Their lips had come together like two magnets, their tongues tasted each other, delving ever deeper, and his hands had stroked the nape of her neck, sending waves of desire zinging through her. He'd held her against his hard body. His heart had thumped against hers. And some sort of promise had been made.

Nothing spoken and nothing specific. But she'd climbed out of his truck on shaky legs, wanting more.

A niggle of doubt crept into her mind, wondering if she was moving too fast with Shane, if this was as good as she thought it was. But she tamped it down, unwilling to lose the glow from his kiss. She was going to trust him and herself.

Her phone rang, and she stretched before answering.

"Good morning," she said, her voice soft.

"Mornin'." Shane's voice was sleep roughened and sent shivers along her spine. "Are you up for a little horseback riding and picnic? With me and Brady, in case I wasn't clear."

His rumble of laughter made her smile.

"I'd love that. What time should I be ready?"

"Right now," he said. "I miss you. However—" he stretched, and the sound carried across the phone "—I suppose I could wait until eleven. At the latest."

Laughing, she sat up in bed. "I'll be there."

At exactly eleven, she turned into Shane's driveway and shut off her engine. Shane and Brady were standing outside, picnic basket at their feet. The little boy was jumping and running around, as if he'd been waiting too long and needed to release some of his energy. Or maybe he was always like this.

But Shane... *Wow.* Energy radiated from him. It was similar to Brady's, yet more contained. Like if he held a plug, he could power a small appliance.

By the time she stepped out of her car, he'd moved to right beside her door.

"Hey," he said, his voice low. "Good timing."

He devoured her with his eyes. She homed in on his mouth, wishing she could kiss him hello, but unsure what to do in front of Brady.

"Naomi, can you believe we're going horseback riding? Dad says I can ride my own horse, instead of riding with him! I can't wait, can you?"

Brady had broken the spell, and she turned to him with a laugh. "I know, it's so exciting! I can't wait to see how well you ride."

The little boy puffed out his chest. "I've been riding forever. How about you? Can you ride?"

She nodded. "I can. I love horses." She knelt down to his level. "I used to ride all the time when I was your age."

"Did you hear that, Dad? She loves horses. Just like we do."

"Really?" Shane led her to his truck. "I didn't know that."

"I never had my own horse," she confided, "but I helped out at the local stables near where I lived growing up."

"Then you're going to love today." He closed her door and climbed into the driver's seat. "Brady, seat belt?"

"Got it, Dad."

Shane gave him a thumbs-up before driving over to the stables. Naomi's heart squeezed. A sense of belonging wrapped around her like her Bubbe's favorite shawl. Through the short drive to the stables and the saddling of the horses, Brady kept up a steady stream of chatter. He didn't appear to need any answers, but Naomi tried to respond as much as possible. She never realized how inquisitive a six-year-old's brain was. Shane winked at her, filling her with delicious warmth as she mounted Pecan and got ready to follow Shane and Brady onto the trail.

The beautiful Texas sunshine warmed her neck as she adjusted to the mare's gait. The temperature was perfect in spring, warm but not too hot. Scents of magnolia blossoms and morning glories filled her nostrils. Birds chirped, now that Brady was quiet as he concentrated on riding his pony.

It was the perfect way to spend a day.

They rode along the lake. The sun reflected off the water, illuminating a pair of wood ducks floating nearby. Cottonwood trees swayed in the light breeze.

"Can we swim, Dad?" Brady asked.

"It's a little cold for that, kiddo."

"Aw, nuts."

"Maybe we can come back in the summer," Naomi said. She tensed, and her horse's gait changed. Focusing on loosening her muscles, she continued. "I don't know if there's a swimming hole over here, or docks, but if so, it would be fun."

"Yeah, Dad, in the summer? Please?"

Shane turned around, his hand in his lap, loosely holding the reins. He grinned at her. "I think that's a great idea."

Summer was a couple months away, and Shane's smile filled her with anticipation. For the first time since she and Andrew broke up, she looked forward to the future with joy. Nothing was going to go wrong this time.

"Hold up." Shane reined in his horse before extending an arm to Brady to make sure he stopped as well, but the pony he was on, Bluebonnet, was happy to do anything the other horses did. Naomi stopped, too. The three of them dismounted.

Shane handed the blanket to Naomi. She looked around the area. Riverbank on the right, cottonwood trees on the left and a low flat spot nearby where they could sit and eat lunch. While Shane and Brady secured the horses, she opened the picnic basket and set everything out— sandwiches, chips, beer and water. Plus, the cookies she'd brought. She set out plates and napkins for everyone, and by then, Shane and Brady finished and sat on the blanket near her. Brady scooted over and pointed to the spot next to her. "You need to sit there, Dad."

"Oh really?" He arched a brow, his mouth quirking.

He nodded. "Nice and close. And look, Dad, Naomi brought cookies!" He gave a big grin.

"They're my grandma's secret recipe," she told him, "and they're delicious."

Before Brady responded, Shane reached for them and put them back in the basket. "After lunch, bud."

Brady's shoulders slumped in the exaggerated way of six-year-olds, and Naomi stifled a laugh. Poor thing. She remembered when the worst thing that could happen in her world was having to eat dessert *after* a meal instead of beforehand.

"Don't worry, Brady," she said. "I made sure to bring plenty."

When they finished eating—and after Brady and Shane had both expressed their love for Naomi's cookies—Brady got up and walked to the river edge. Keeping one eye on his son, Shane leaned closer to Naomi.

"Think Brady would notice if I kissed you right now?" Shane asked, keeping his voice low.

His tone, and the suggestion, shot straight to her core. Shane must have noticed because his pupils dilated.

"Unfortunately, I think he would," she said. "You've got a very smart son. Although based on his continued throwing us together, I don't think he'd mind."

"Hmm." His tone was a mix of disappointment and pride, and Naomi laughed.

"Dad, Naomi, look at this!" Brady ran over, his hands

filled with quartzite, sandstone and limestone rocks. "They're so cool."

Naomi admired them before choosing a smooth flat one buried among the others in his grimy hand. "Do you mind if I take this?" she asked.

Brady nodded, and she walked to the river's edge and threw it in the water.

"Hey, wa— Wow, look at that!"

The rock skipped four times across the water.

"How did you do that?" Brady asked. "Can I try?" He took one of the rocks he'd collected and threw it in the water. It sank.

"I can teach you," she said. "First, though, it has to be the right kind of rock. Did you see how I took one of your smooth ones? That's the kind you need."

Brady's eyes lit up. He dumped the rocks he'd found and ran around the river's edge, collecting smooth rocks. Shane came up behind her as Brady approached.

"What about these?" the little boy asked, holding both grubby hands cupped around a pile of stones.

Studying his selection, Naomi chose one and nodded. "This is a good one. Here, feel the weight of it?"

He handed his pile to his dad and took the rock from Naomi. "Sort of."

"You don't want them too heavy or they'll sink. But if they're too light, they won't work either."

"Oh, I see." He looked around and pulled a few more. "How about these?"

"Those are perfect," Naomi said. She curved her finger around the rock. "This is how you hold it."

When he struggled to imitate her, she stood behind him and molded his fingers. "Like this…"

Then she took his arm, swung it back and to the side and

made the motion he'd need to throw the rock. "You're going to do it like this. Not over your head and not underhanded. But kind of sideways so the rock has a chance to skim."

He tried and failed. Biting his lip, he tried again. He went through the entire pile of rocks he'd collected.

Naomi expected him to give up in frustration, but instead, he searched for more rocks. When one skipped once, he jumped up and down, whooping.

"I did it, I did it!" His glee was contagious, and Naomi cheered him on.

"You sure did! That was awesome."

"Dad, can you do it?"

Shane stepped forward. "I haven't done it in a long time." He turned to Naomi with a rueful smile. "I think we're going to be here awhile."

Joy filled her. "That's fine with me."

Together, the three of them collected skipping rocks before deciding to have a contest. Once they each had a small pile, they stood at the water's edge. Brady went first. His rock skipped twice. Then Shane, whose rock skipped three times. Naomi's rock skipped seven.

Shock shone from the boy's eyes. Shane's were filled with admiration. "You're full of surprises," he said.

Naomi grinned. "I was always good at this."

"Again," Brady insisted.

This time, his rock skipped three times and tied with his dad, but Naomi still beat them both with six.

"This is so cool!" Brady exclaimed. "Wait until I tell my friends at school. They're going to want to meet you," he said, turning to Naomi.

"I'd love to meet them," she replied. "And if they want to learn, I'd be happy to show them." She got serious then.

"But you have to promise not to come near the water without your dad's permission, okay?"

Shane nodded solemnly at his son. "That's right. The same water rules apply, even when skipping rocks."

Brady looked between his dad and Naomi. "I've got it. No going to the water without asking Mom or Dad. Or Kevin or Naomi, right?" His eyes gleamed, and her heart hitched at being included in his list of trusted adults.

"That's right," Shane said.

Brady tugged at Shane's shirt, and when he leaned down, said, "Dad, you should marry her!"

Shane tousled his hair before putting his arm around Naomi. The weight and warmth felt good, and she leaned into him. "He likes you," he whispered, his mouth near her ear as Brady returned his attention to the rocks. His breath heated her skin and blew strands of her hair.

"I like him, too," she said, her voice quiet.

He pulled her close, their sides touching. His chest expanded and contracted with each breath he took. She stood in the moment, watching Brady play, listening to the nature sounds around them, and feeling Shane's hard, muscular body against hers. Peace settled over her.

This was what she'd always wanted. She'd searched for it, and then assumed she had it with Andrew. But in reality, she'd always been chasing the feeling of belonging, sure that it was to be found in a few more weeks' time, after a holiday gathering, or the next time he told her he loved her. The goalpost always moved though.

But with Shane—and Brady—she didn't have to worry about "next time." *They* were the goalposts.

"Are you going to kiss her, Dad?"

Naomi startled at the sound of Brady's voice, and Shane's

body shook with suppressed laughter. Rather than letting her go, he held her tighter.

"I'm thinking about it, kiddo," he said. His fingers strummed her side, sending chills around her torso.

Brady groaned. "Okay, fine. Kevin kisses Mom, too. I guess it's okay."

"What about you?" he asked Naomi, his blue eyes crinkling with humor. "Is it okay with you?"

He'd turned to face away from his son, and the humor slowly turned to tenderness, deepening his eyes to navy.

She slid her arms around his waist and leaned against him. "Yes," she whispered.

Without giving her a chance to say anything else, he lowered his head and touched his mouth to hers. His kiss was warm and firm, their breaths mingling as one. She sighed against him, and he held her tighter, stroking her waist with his fingers. Each touch sent a trail of fire to her core.

Too soon, he pulled away from her. Resting his forehead against hers, he exhaled. "If you only knew how badly I've longed to kiss you all day, how I want to extend this longer even now, you'd probably run away," he said, his voice low, his eyes dark with desire.

She gave a shaky laugh. "I'm really not a runner, so you'd probably catch me pretty quickly."

He gazed at her, his eyes lightening with humor. "As much as I love having my son around, I don't think any of us are prepared for more right now."

Her desire for this man, to belong to someone completely, was overridden by the practical side of the moment. Brady was six years old, and there was only so much she was willing to do in front of a child.

Clearing her throat, she stepped away from Shane. "Next time," she promised.

Shane's nostrils flared. He pinned her with a longing look and walked away, cleaning up their picnic detritus and calling to Brady to get ready to leave.

If she hadn't heard the hitch in his breath, she never would suspect how much he'd hated to turn away. As it was, his ability to act unfazed astounded her. Her entire body tingled, and all she wanted was to take that kiss further. *Deeper.* But as he'd told her, it was neither the time nor the place, something she'd have to adjust to if she wanted a family guy.

She did.

Today convinced her.

"Okay, Brady," Shane said later that week as he pulled off the main road in Emerald Ridge. "Remember, you're going to be in Naomi's grandma's home, so you have to listen and not make a mess. Got it?"

A trickle of sweat ran down the back of his neck as he steered his truck into the parking space behind the garden apartment complex and prepared to unleash his energetic little boy into the living quarters of Naomi's grandmother.

So many things could go wrong. His brain spun with disaster scenarios worthy of a dystopian novel. His son could easily break something, for that matter. Naomi had told him how the apartment had to be deep cleaned for the holiday. What if Brady had a cookie in his pocket?

"Hey, Brady, you didn't bring any food with you, did you?"

His son looked at him cross-eyed. "No."

Well, that was one less thing that could go wrong. But seriously, didn't old ladies keep fragile stuff all around? Heck, *they* were fragile with old bones. What if Brady knocked her over?

"Remember, no running."

"I know, Dad."

Still, the kid fidgeted all the time, including now.

He needed to relax. Shane was about to ring the doorbell when he froze. He'd been so busy worrying about Brady, he'd forgotten to worry about himself.

What if the grandmother didn't like him?

"Dad, ring the doorbell."

He winced at his son's loud voice. Too late to worry now. Especially because he'd barely raised his hand to ring said doorbell when the door flew open.

And now he couldn't breathe. Because Naomi stood there, joy suffusing her face.

"Hi." Her voice was warm and sent shards of relief through him.

"Hi, Naomi!" Brady cried. He jumped forward and gave her a hug.

Her eyes widened, a look of shock briefly crossing her face before she hugged him back. "I'm so happy to see you, Brady. Come on in, both of you."

"Naomi, you need to explain to my dad that I know how to behave. He thinks I'm going to destroy your grandma's house." He lowered his voice. "I only make a mess in my room."

Shane's embarrassment switched to humor, and he laughed along with Naomi.

"Guess we haven't mastered discretion," he told her.

"Come on in and meet my grandma," she murmured, squeezing Shane's hand and pulling him into the sunny living room.

"Wait," he said, pulling her toward him. "Can I give you a kiss hello first?"

She nodded, and he bent his head and gently kissed

her lips. The last of his nerves evaporated. "Okay, introduce us."

She led them inside, where her grandmother had already risen from the sofa and was waiting for them.

"Grandma, this is Shane and Brady. Shane, Brady, this is my grandmother."

She stepped forward, her face creased in a smile. "You can call me Sophie or Bubbe. I'm so happy to meet you both. And, Brady," she said, turning to him, "don't worry about making a mess. It never killed anyone as far as I know."

Brady smiled. "Well, maybe if my toys were so high they toppled over."

Bubbe laughed. "Very true. But I don't think you're going to do that here, are you?"

"Nah, it's too hard to clean them up."

"I probably should warn you that Brady is really, really shy," Shane said, ruffling his son's hair.

"Must take after you," Bubbe retorted with a wink. "Can I get anyone drinks?"

Naomi's grandmother looked like an older version of Naomi, especially when she smiled. Despite her white hair, her face had only traces of wrinkles and her movements were spry. He didn't have to worry his son would destroy the woman.

He also got a good hint at what Naomi would look like as she aged, and it intrigued him. Because while she was beautiful now, he had a feeling she'd only get better with age.

Bubbe gestured to the granite counter separating the kitchen from the living area, where a pitcher of sweet tea and four glasses sat.

"Brady, if you'd rather water or something else, just tell me and I'll make sure you've got it. Plus—" she leaned down toward him "—there's food, too, so let me know if you're hungry."

"Dad said we're baking."

Naomi nodded. "We're baking Passover treats. My favorites!"

"I like treats." Brady gave a gap-toothed smile.

Everybody laughed.

"I know you do," Naomi said. "I do, too. So I'm glad you're here. Want to help me get set up?"

The little boy nodded, and with an admonishment from Shane to wash his hands, he followed Naomi into the kitchen.

Meanwhile, her grandma patted the blue and silver upholstered sofa. "That granddaughter of mine has a sweet tooth like nobody's business. Shane, come sit down," she said. He joined her, feeling a little like a schoolboy being sent to the principal's office. "Do you know anything about Passover?"

He wasn't expecting that question. He'd been prepared for questions about his background or family or his job. Or even Brady and his ex-wife. But Passover?

"Not really," he confessed.

"It commemorates Moses leading the Israelites out of Egypt," she explained. "It's an eight-day holiday of freedom, and during that time, we only eat unleavened bread or bread products. So to prepare, we have to clean our house and cook special foods. We have a celebratory dinner where we recite the story of the holiday. Naomi and I, and now you and Brady, are going to make some desserts for the seder and for during the week."

"I appreciate being invited to help out," he said.

She patted his knee. "This is about more than helping. It's about *belonging*." She glanced toward the kitchen, a soft smile on her face.

He followed her gaze. Naomi and Brady were spreading chocolate on top of matzah crackers, the two of them giggling together.

The older woman continued. "You two are more alike than you realize, but there are some major issues." She pressed her lips together.

His mind immediately went to their different religions. He'd always celebrated holidays with his family. He enjoyed the family gathering together and the fun traditions he and his siblings and cousins practiced, like Secret Santa at Christmas, and turning the Easter egg hunt into an Olympic-level contest of who could find the most eggs first.

"I'm happy to learn about Judaism," he said, realizing he meant it as the words exited his mouth. "And to introduce her to my customs, too."

Bubbe smiled. "That's wonderful to hear, but I'm also concerned about her inability to have children. Her ex destroyed her belief in herself. Have you two discussed what her infertility means for your future?" She leaned away from Shane, folding her arms across her stomach.

He turned once again toward the kitchen. Brady's hands were chocolatey, as was his cheek. He started to rise, but Bubbe put a hand on his knee.

"Leave them be," she said. "Naomi can handle it."

Naomi *could* handle a lot of things. Including his messy son. He was starting to realize that. He exhaled.

Cocking her head to the side, she continued. "If you haven't—and even if you have—you should discuss again what you want for your family. She was hurt once before, and I don't want to see that happen again."

"You're right," he said. "We do need to discuss it. I guess I assumed we could work things out as we went along."

Her voice strained. "I'm sure you two could, but it's often

easier to be clear from the beginning about what each of you wants, needs and expects."

"You're right," Shane said. "Again."

Bubbe's eyes glowed with a mischievous glimmer. She leaned around Shane and called out to Naomi. "Naomi, I like this man!"

Shane's neck heated, and Naomi whipped her head around.

"Excuse me?" She paused what she and Brady were doing and looked between her grandmother and him, making Shane feel even more under a spotlight. "What did I miss?"

Cackling, the woman patted Shane's knee before walking over to the kitchen. "He told me I'm right."

Shane laughed quietly to himself and followed Bubbe.

"Right about what?" Naomi asked.

"Doesn't matter," her grandmother responded. "All that matters is that he's my new favorite."

"What about me?" Brady asked, eyes downcast.

Bubbe rushed over and gave him a hug. Shane loved her for ignoring his son's chocolate stains.

"You're also my favorite," she said. "Especially because you've just learned how to make my favorite Passover snack...which I just realized needs a better name."

"What was it called?" Shane asked.

Naomi shook her head at him, then whispered, "Tell you later." Raising her voice, she said, "Bubbe's right...it needs a good name. Brady, what should we call this?" She pointed to the pieces of matzah covered in chocolate, caramel and salt. How could something that good not already have a name? And if it did, why wasn't Naomi answering him?

"I think it should be called matzah sticky crumble," Brady said.

Naomi's and her grandmother's eyes lit up. "That's the perfect name," Bubbe said.

"I love it," Naomi answered.

"Brady, come on over to the sink and let me help you clean your face and hands," Bubbe told him.

While the two of them battled the soap, Naomi slipped over to Shane. "The actual name is matzah crack, because you can't stop eating it, but that's not exactly kid friendly," she murmured.

He started to laugh, but stifled it when Brady looked over at him. "Dad, you should kiss her," he called.

He and Naomi automatically stepped apart. Bubbe's shoulders shook with silent laughter, and Naomi closed her eyes.

"Give it a rest, Brady." He shot his son a warning look. "We're baking, *not* kissing."

"Mom and Kevin can do both," he argued. "Besides, Bubbe needs to know how much you like each other, don't you, Bubbe?"

"You, my little man, are a troublemaker," the older woman said. "Let's dry your hands and get back to Passover baking." She glanced over at Shane and Naomi. "And you two, if you want to kiss or not, that's fine with me, but first clean up the matzah crumbs. They're everywhere. It looks like a Passover glitter bomb exploded."

Naomi's face was beet red, and she focused her gaze on the counter. Shane walked over to her, placed a hand on her shoulder and whispered in her ear. "Your grandma is awesome."

Turning toward him, she leaned her head against his shoulder. By now, Bubbe had ushered Brady out of the kitchen. Shane didn't know where his son was, but it didn't matter. Not in this moment. So he wrapped his arms around Naomi and stood there, waiting to see what would happen.

"She can be a lot," Naomi whispered back, looking up at him.

He shrugged. "I can handle it."

"What were you discussing on the sofa?"

This wasn't the time or the place to get into a big conversation, but he wasn't about to lie to Naomi either. "Our future."

She blanched. "I'm sorry."

He shook his head. "Don't be."

Bubbe's voice interrupted them, again. "Are you as eager to learn about Passover as you are to clean? Because not only are they related, but you don't seem to be doing much of it, you two."

"Yes, Bubbe, we're cleaning," Naomi said with a sigh.

Winking, they cleaned up the work area.

"We're finished," Naomi called out to her grandma. "What are we making, now?"

"How about the applesauce kugel," Bubbe suggested.

She and the little boy came back into the kitchen and pulled out pots and pans while Naomi grabbed the ingredients. Shane and Brady got to work following the recipe, and soon, all four were working in tandem. By the time they put the two pans of applesauce kugel into the oven to bake, they had a method established that made Shane feel as if the four of them had been cooking forever.

"Do you two always do all the baking for Passover?" he asked as they took a brief break.

Naomi looked at her grandmother with love. "It's kind of our special thing, but we aren't the only ones who do it. My grandma hosts, but everyone else brings things, too. We just like doing this together."

"I love baking," Brady said. "I think I'm going to be a baker when I grow up."

"That's awesome." Naomi's eyes were bright.

Shane loved how encouraging she was of his son.

"What's going to be your specialty?" she asked, drying her hands on the bluebird-printed dish towel and hopping up on the stool next to Brady.

His son scrunched his face, giving serious thought to the question, which only made Shane more eager to hear the answer.

"I think… I want to make cookies. And cakes."

Shane nodded. "I love both of those things, so I approve." He patted his stomach, making everyone laugh.

"I'm not just going to bake for you, Dad. I'm going to have a store." His eyes widened. "Like Rosa!"

Naomi's smile disappeared, her eyes widened and she glanced at her grandmother. "Oh no, did you place an order for Passover chocolates with Abuela Rosa? I totally forgot."

Bubbe patted her arm. "Of course I did," the old woman said. "It's on my list."

She pointed to the refrigerator, where several lined papers were attached with tape.

"Thank goodness," Naomi said, sagging a little in her seat. "I love how she makes us special chocolate every Passover. I can't decide which would be worse, not having it for our seder, or her thinking we didn't like it anymore."

"Not to worry, *bubbelah*. That's why I keep such comprehensive Passover lists. And especially, with her business struggling, I wanted to make sure to request it early."

Bubbe smiled almost wistfully. "The first time she did it was years ago. My husband had stopped by her stand." She directed her story to Brady. "When she first started making chocolate, she sold some of it at a roadside stand.

Anyway," she continued, "he stopped by because he knew how much I loved chocolate. Her confections became my favorite, and he always bought me some for my birthday. But one year, my birthday fell during Passover. And when she heard we couldn't eat it during the holiday, she offered to make us a special Passover kind. She researched the ingredients and everything. So now, we buy it every year for our seder." She shook her head. "It just wouldn't be Passover without her chocolate."

Naomi slipped off her stool and gave her grandmother a hug. "I never knew that's how it started."

She dabbed her eyes. "Yes. And that's why Abuela Rosa Chocolate is always on my Passover list."

"I could make special Passover cookies and cakes," Brady announced, bouncing in his seat. "That way everyone could eat my treats."

"That's a lovely idea," Naomi said. "But you should also make others for the rest of the year, so that everyone will want to eat them."

"Who's hungry?" Bubbe asked as she pulled the kugels out of the oven.

"I am!" Brady sniffed. "They smell so good!"

"Don't they?" Bubbe rested them on the stove. "All that cinnamon is heavenly. But these are going to get frozen. However, this one is okay for us to eat."

Shane frowned at the small pan that she pointed to. "I don't remember making that one," he said.

"That's because you didn't," Naomi explained. "My grandmother feeds everyone. So she made a small one ahead of time, knowing that we'd all be hungry and need a snack. Right, Bubbe?"

"Of course. It's against the law not to feed people," she

claimed. "I'm pretty sure it says so on the Ten Commandments."

"Dad, is that true?"

Shane laughed and ruffled his son's hair. "I think she's joking, kiddo, but just in case she isn't, we should eat."

Bubbe brought the small kugel into the dining room and served everyone at the table on paper plates. "Make sure to let it cool," she said, eyeing Brady.

Shane appreciated how everyone was looking out for his son and including him in all parts of the activity.

Because the maple table was small and square, each of them sat on one side of it. Shane wished Naomi was closer to him. He'd watched her all afternoon, admiring her way with Brady and her grandmother, but wanting some time with her to himself. Since that wasn't possible, he'd hoped they could at least sit next to each other. But with this configuration, the only thing he'd be able to do was play footsie with her beneath the table, and there was too much of a chance he'd end up playing with someone else's foot.

So he banked his frustration and enjoyed the opportunity to act like a whole family.

He took a mouthful of kugel.

Was this what life could be like if he and Naomi got together? Although this was his first time doing anything for Passover, he felt like he fit in. He loved learning about new things, and if the rest of the food was anything like this kugel, he'd happily eat it.

"This is delicious," he praised. "I had no idea you could turn matzah into this."

Naomi laughed. "With enough applesauce, cinnamon and sugar, it's almost possible to forget about what you're missing."

"I didn't know we were going to get to eat the food we

made," Brady said with his mouth full. "Dad was wrong. He said to make sure I didn't ask to eat anything."

Leave it to a six-year-old to say the quiet parts out loud.

"I also told you to mind your manners, bud, and you're talking with food in your mouth."

Brady swallowed and everyone laughed.

"They're so nice, they won't mind," the boy said.

"Oh, look at this one, buttering me up," Bubbe said. She squeezed his shoulders, her eyes bright with laughter. "And it's working, too."

He gave a gap-toothed smile. "See?"

"Clearly, he's intimidated by you all," Shane said to their laughter. "I hate to break this up, but we've got to get going. Brady has a doctor's appointment."

"Do I *have* to go?" Brady whined. "It's so much fun here."

"You do, buddy, sorry."

Sighing from his toes like only children can, Brady rose and brought his plate into the kitchen. Naomi's grandmother raised her eyebrows. "You taught him well."

"Thanks," Shane said, pride warming him. "His mother and I agreed on raising him with good manners."

Rising, he took the remaining empty plates into the kitchen before helping Brady with his jacket. Then he turned to Naomi. "I had a great time," he said, cupping her cheek. "Thanks for inviting us." He kissed her, quicker than he would have liked, but there were others around.

"It was great having you here. Thanks for your help, Brady," she called to him.

The boy ran over and gave her a hug, as well as her grandmother. "I had fun."

"Come over this evening?" Shane asked.

Naomi paused before nodding her head.

Satisfied, he turned to Bubbe. "Thank you for including us. It was great meeting you." He leaned down and lowered his voice. "And I will give serious consideration to what we discussed."

She stood on tiptoe and kissed his cheek. "Anytime. And thank you for your help. And for listening to my concerns."

Shane ushered Brady out the door, wishing he could stay longer. He'd enjoyed himself, but there hadn't been enough alone time with Naomi. He sighed, knowing there would be time tonight and searching for the patience to wait that long.

"You really should marry her, Dad," Brady declared as Shane waited for him to buckle his seat belt.

The comment caught him off guard. It shouldn't have, since Brady clearly had fallen in love with Naomi. Just as Shane paid attention to Naomi and Brady's interactions, clearly Brady had done the same with his dad's.

"You really think so, huh?"

An emphatic nod from his son made Shane smile.

"She's awesome. And I'd get another grandmother, too."

Brady paused, counting out all his grandparents on his fingers.

"Kevin's mom and dad live far away in a nursing home, so I don't get to see them. And Mom's parents don't live around here either. But Naomi and Bubbe live right here, just like Grandma and Grandpa do! I could visit all the time."

Driving down the roads of Emerald Ridge, Shane listened as Brady extolled the virtues of having more grandparents. His son was really embracing the idea of Naomi becoming part of his family. It warmed Shane's heart, but also scared him a little. His son was moving fast, falling in love with Naomi almost faster than Shane had. Which was great, but what if the relationship didn't work out? The last thing he wanted was to hurt his son.

"I'm glad you like Naomi and her grandmother, bud. Let's just slow down though." Rushing things was never the way to go.

Brady scrunched his face in confusion as he climbed out of the truck at the doctor's office. "Why? You like Naomi, don't you?"

Shane nodded. He more than liked her. And he thought she felt the same way. But her grandmother was right. Before they went any further, they needed to talk.

"She likes you, too. I saw her looking at you with that lovey-dovey look on her face." Brady grinned as he spoke, obviously loving the opportunity to tell his dad what to do.

Shane humored him.

"I saw it, too," he admitted. He'd have had to be blind to miss the signs of attraction.

He'd caught her staring at him at odd times as they made the Passover treats. She'd bit her lip, eyes darkening, when she looked at him. She played with her hair, and touched him more than usual.

"So then, what's the waiting for? You don't want her to fall in love with someone else, do you?"

Shane's heart seized. "No, I don't." Did she realized how he felt about her?

Shrugging, Brady reached for the door of the medical office. "I don't get grown-ups."

And this time, Shane totally agreed with his son. It was time to get moving.

That evening, Naomi stood on the steps of Shane's home, shifting from one foot to the other. He'd asked her to come over, and she'd been looking forward to tonight. Her mind had been occupied by him, rather than on cleaning up after their baking session today.

Her grandmother had noticed her distraction, and as usual, had known the exact source of her daydreams. She'd teased her gently, and even kvelled over Brady and how great he was. But this time, something in her tone had been off. Her voice had been strained, her posture tense. Naomi hadn't been able to put her finger on what it was, and when she'd asked, Bubbe had said she was tired from all the activity.

It made sense, but in the back of her mind, the worry remained.

She rang Shane's doorbell, listening to the chime echo inside the house. As Shane's footsteps indicated he was approaching, she glanced at her phone again. She'd made her grandmother promise to call her if she needed anything, and as of now, there was no message. She hoped a good night's sleep would cure whatever ailed the older woman.

"Hello, beautiful," Shane said, pulling the door open and taking her in his arms.

She leaned into him, overcome by his warm presence, minty scent and powerful body that wrapped her up and made her feel like she'd never come to any harm.

It made her dreams seem real.

She pulled away. "Hi." Her voice came out shy, even to her own ears.

Shane stared at her, taking in her ponytail, navy sweater, faded jeans and tennis shoes. His gaze roved back up, but not without leaving a trail of heat along her entire body.

She gulped.

Seeming to get ahold of himself, he backed up and welcomed her inside. Despite the warmer temperatures during the day, the night was cool and a fire blazed in the fireplace, the flickering flames casting an orange glow in the large room. Shane had dimmed the lights and lit large pillar candles. It was romantic and cozy, a direct contrast to this afternoon's bustling activities at her grandmother's.

Taking her hand, he led her over to the sofa and pulled her onto his lap.

"I feel like I haven't seen you in ages," he said, making circular motions on her back.

She took his other hand in hers, enjoying the firm clasp of their fingers around each other. "It's only been a few hours."

"Yes, but during those few hours, I took Brady to his doctor's appointment, chatted about stuff that's important to a six-year-old—did you know that certain species of frogs can freeze almost solid in winter and defrost like nothing happened in the spring?"

Naomi laughed. "No, can't say that I did. Where is Brady, by the way?"

"Sleeping at his mom's house. And before those few hours apart from you, we hung out with your grandma and Brady, which I loved, don't get me wrong, but I couldn't exactly kiss you in front of them."

"My grandma probably would have cheered you on," Naomi said with a smile.

"Not if I kissed you like this."

He turned her to face him, straddling her legs on either side of his thighs. Taking her face in his hands, he devoured her mouth, pouring all of his frustration at their separation into the kiss.

Naomi wrapped her arms around his neck, pressed her chest against his and kissed him back just as fiercely.

His heart beat against her chest, and he moaned as their tongues met and tussled with each other. He nibbled her bottom lip, the pull causing her to ache. She ran her hands through his short hair. Her need for him built, but he pulled away. She whimpered when he released her mouth, only to trail kisses down her neck. She shivered at his heated contact and bent her head away to give him more access. When he reached her collarbone, he pulled at her sweater and then paused, looking at her for permission.

She nodded before grasping the hem of her top and yanking it over her head.

His sharp intake of breath, his clear appreciation of her body, filled her with pride and power. Naomi loved having this effect on him. She straightened her shoulders, and his pupils dilated as he looked at her. Grasping her waist, he kissed his way down to her breasts, licking the lace edge of her bra. Heat spiraled through her body, coiling around her. She ran her hands down to his shoulders, slipping her fingers between the gaps of his button-down shirt.

A muttered *mmm-hmm* was all she needed to hear. She unbuttoned his shirt, pushing it down over his biceps. He freed his hands from the confines of the cloth before trying to return to her breasts. Except now it was her turn. She stopped him, forcing him to remain upright as she admired the tightness of his chest and abs, the hard planes and defined muscles turning her insides to jelly.

"Enough." His strained, roughened voice was all the warning she received before he took her in his arms and rose from the sofa. She wrapped her legs around his waist as his long strides brought them in front of the fireplace. He laid her gently down on the soft rug and sat beside her.

"The sofa is too small for me to explore your body the way it was meant to be explored," he rasped.

Desire flooded her. She didn't know if it was the sight of the flames turning his sculpted chest bronze, the words he spoke or the tone of his voice, but she wanted him. More than she'd ever anticipated. More than she probably should.

She was tired of fighting against what her body and her heart told her. She rose onto her knees and pulled him toward her, until their chests touched, skin to skin.

His fingers clasped her bra strap. "May I?"

She nodded, pressing her mouth to his. As their tongues danced once again, he removed her bra, sliding it out from between them. The friction of lace against skin made her nipples pucker even more than the contact with his body, and she pushed against him. His belt buckle prodded against her stomach, the cold metal against her warm skin focusing her attention on that one spot. But below the buckle pressed against her, too, sending sparks of desire zinging through her body.

Unwilling to break contact with his mouth, she slid her arms between them and tried to unbuckle his belt by feel. Each time her fingers dipped between his jeans and his stomach, his skin jumped.

"Stop," he growled. He moved her hands away, pulling back so their lips separated, and made quick work of unbuckling his belt.

"You're tormenting me," he said, voice hoarse.

She grinned, leaning back on an elbow to watch him. "You're *tantalizing* me."

He shut his eyes for a brief moment before opening the fly of his jeans and shimmying out of them, fumbling with the pocket before throwing the jeans to the side.

"I'll give you tantalizing…" He crawled slowly toward her until he loomed over her body, eyes dark with need.

He remained there, pinning her with his stare but not touching her, giving her a chance to get away.

She didn't want to run. She wanted this incredibly sexy man right now.

"Please do," she whispered.

He sat back on his haunches and reached for her jeans. "May I?"

She'd never thought of those two words as scintillating before, but when Shane said them? Oh my.

"Yes."

It was the last coherent thought she had as he kissed her out of her clothes. By the time she was naked, every inch of her craved him. And her insides? She thought they'd explode if he didn't enter her right this second.

He picked up the condom packet he'd removed from his jeans pocket and held it between his teeth as he removed his boxers.

Oh no, she wasn't letting him have all the fun. Swiping it from his mouth, she tore it open. Then slowly—maddeningly slowly, if his breathing was any indication—she rolled it onto him. When she finished, she looked into his eyes.

He wrapped his arms around her and lowered them both to the rug. Her body vibrated with desire for him. But he wasn't yet ready. He started by her feet, kissing his way around each ankle before sliding up the calf of one leg and the thigh of the other. He gave her a wicked grin, and her insides clenched at what he could possibly do.

"Later," he whispered, his breath hot on her skin. He slid his body against hers until their mouths met.

If he thought she was going to lie here quietly, though, he was wrong. As he braced himself above her, she slid down his body, leaving a trail of kisses in her wake. He groaned each time she touched him, each time she teased him, until she wasn't sure who was more turned on.

"Naomi." Her name came out as a groan, as a plea, and finally, she crawled back to where she'd started.

They locked eyes, and he entered her slowly, carefully, teasing and drawing out the inevitable bliss they both coveted. Her breath caught in her chest, her body trembled, and she reached for him, needing him to be inside her. Finally, with one long thrust, he entered. As if they'd been together for years, their bodies rocked in tandem, climbing toward their release. Her lungs burned, her muscles clenched and her climax rolled through her like a freight train. She screamed his name at almost the same time he shouted hers. Stars burst behind her eyelids, and their hearts pounded out a maniacal rhythm together as they came down.

As they lay together, limbs tangled, skin sweat-slicked, breaths mingling, the only thought Naomi could hold on to was how electric their passion was. Never before had she been so carried away. For all her confidence in doling out advice, she'd never felt so empowered during sex. She drifted along in the afterglow, gratification and contentment warming her body. Shane's fingers traced lazy circles along her hip. Her heart rate slowed, and a delicious lethargy consumed her. The smoky scent of the fire, the soft plush of the rug beneath her and the weight of Shane's body against her helped her doze. When at last she opened her eyes, she met his gentle gaze.

"Hey, beautiful," he whispered.

Her cheeks heated. "Hey."

"That was absolutely incredible."

It was. So incredible, in fact, she didn't know how to put into words all of her feelings. Honestly, she wasn't even sure what those feelings were, other than amazement. Although, all the signs had been there. Every time they'd been together, that pull of attraction, the instant spark of chemistry, had grabbed her attention.

"It was amazing," she agreed softly.

He reached for a blanket on the ottoman nearby and spread it out over the two of them. Pillowing her head on his chest, he folded one arm beneath his head while holding her with the other arm.

She liked the cocoon and nestled in.

"I think it's time we make this official," he said.

"I'd like that," she said. "A lot."

The sigh he expelled was the only hint he'd been nervous about her answer.

"Do you think Brady will be okay with it?"

He lifted his head and stared at her, incredulity brightening his eyes. "Are you *kidding* me? He's been after me to make you his stepmom on an almost hourly basis. That kid is besotted with you." He kissed the top of her head. "As am I."

Naomi couldn't keep the grin from spreading across her face. "He's a fantastic kid. Even my grandmother was talking about his intelligence and good behavior."

"Thank God," Shane said. "I was convinced he was going to damage something. Or her."

Laughing, Naomi squeezed his hand. "She's a lot tougher than she looks."

"Yeah, she's actually a little scary."

Naomi pulled away. "What do you mean?" She recalled that afternoon and couldn't think of anything her grandmother had done that could be deemed "scary."

"Maybe *scary* is the wrong word," he clarified. "But she's very protective of you. She wanted to know if we'd discussed our future."

"When did that happen?" Naomi frowned. Her grandmother had done nothing but practically throw Shane in front of her. Why had she shown this other side of herself to him?

"When we first arrived. You and Brady went into the kitchen, and she and I were sitting on the sofa."

Guilt tightened her chest. She'd been so enamored with Brady, she hadn't paid attention to their conversation.

"I'm sorry she did that," Naomi said. "It's unlike her."

"You have no reason to apologize. She made a lot of good points. I'm an adult and can handle it. Besides, she loves you."

"She's never done that with any other guys."

"She knows how big a deal not being able to have kids is to you, and she doesn't want to see you hurt again."

Naomi looked over at him, afraid to ask her question, but knowing she had to. "And what did you say?"

He kissed her. "I don't want you hurt, either. And I agreed communication is important. Especially between you and me."

The bliss Naomi had felt lessened, replaced by a nagging anxiety. Their religious differences could be overcome, but would Shane want more kids someday? It was too early to ask, but at some point, she was going to have to. Her stomach lurched. He wouldn't turn away from her because she couldn't have kids, right? He already knew that about her.

Shane massaged her neck. "Relax," he whispered. "It's going to be fine."

Never in the history of mankind had being told to relax ever worked. Naomi didn't have much hope in its success now. But she was going to try hard to believe. First, though, she had to talk to Bubbe.

Chapter Nine

Shane whistled on his way to work the next day, finally confident his quest to find someone to spend the rest of his life with was heading in the right direction. As he'd suspected, sex with Naomi had been one of the best experiences of his life. Their chemistry was undeniable, and their needs and desires matched. Their emotional connection stunned him. And his heart had raced when she'd eagerly taken charge. He shook his head. On the outside, she appeared totally in command. But she'd fallen apart in his arms and the contradiction was hotter than he'd thought possible.

He glanced at the calla lilies in the passenger seat beside him. Instead of going directly to the office, he was making a quick stop at Naomi's. She deserved beautiful things, and these flowers he'd seen in the shop window had made him think of her. They were elegant with soft petals and a lovely scent. Best of all, they were a deep, dark red, and the variety was actually called "Naomi."

If he'd needed proof the stars were aligned, this was it.

He parked in front of her office and knocked on the door before entering.

Naomi walked toward the front. Her face brightened. "I didn't expect to see you this morning."

He pulled her into his arms and gave her a kiss, wanting it to last for a lot longer than either of them had time for.

"I saw these and thought of you. They're called Naomi Calla Lilies. I couldn't resist."

She laughed, taking them from him and bringing them to her nose. "They're beautiful, thank you. Let me just get something to put them in…" She walked away and came back a moment later with a tall glass vase.

Was this a thing? Did all women just have spare vases hidden away in case someone brought them flowers? Probably not, but his Naomi was prepared for any occasion, even surprise flowers.

His Naomi.

He liked that.

When she'd arranged the flowers to her liking, she returned to him and kissed him again. "Thank you, I'll think of you every time I look at them."

"Can I see you again tonight?"

"I'm working until three and then have to stop at Bubbe's, but after that I'm free."

"How about I pick you up at six thirty and we'll have dinner?"

"Sounds good. With or without Brady?"

He loved how she asked as if it were no big deal. "Without. He's with his mom today." He paused. "I'd better get going."

"Have a good day today." She leaned up and kissed him again. It was sweet and full of promise, and Shane would have given anything to stay in her office. But he had work to do, and even though Naomi was now down one client, he assumed she did, too. With a groan, he pulled away, tipped his hat and left.

For the rest of the day, he couldn't help but look forward

to tonight. No matter what he was doing, Naomi was forefront in his mind. When he spoke to the ranch hands, he wondered what clients she was helping today. When he ate lunch, he thought about their dinner tonight and whether to take her to a restaurant or bring something in at home. And when Lacey texted him about Brady, he remembered how awesome Naomi was with his son.

By the time the end of his workday arrived, and it was time to go home, shower and change, he was practically humming with excitement. Just as he pulled into his driveway, his phone rang. A huge grin spread across his face.

"Hey, Naomi, are you as excited to see me as I am you?" He climbed out of his car and loped into the house.

"That's actually what I'm calling about."

He stopped, halfway between his mudroom and kitchen. He heard no excitement in her voice.

"I can't get together tonight after all," she said.

He dropped onto the shoe bench. "Is everything all right?"

"Yeah. Look, I'm sorry, but something's come up and tonight's just not going to work."

"Maybe tomorrow?"

She gave some noncommittal answer before saying she had to go.

"Sure." He was about to ask if there was anything he could do, or how her day went, or anything really to keep her talking to him, but the call disconnected. He sat where he was for a few moments, looking at his phone, stunned.

What had happened between this morning and now?

Disappointment washed over him. Shaking his head, he went to fix himself something to eat, all appetite gone. The evening stretched ahead of him, though, his unwanted freedom mocking him.

* * *

Naomi sat in her dark apartment, shaking. She stared at her phone and reminded herself she'd done the right thing. She'd fallen hard and fast for Shane, and the depth and strength of her feelings terrified her.

After leaving Shane's last evening, she'd spent most of the night awake, analyzing every aspect of their day—Passover cooking, her conversations with Brady and, of course, sex with Shane.

Everything had been perfect. The family baking activity had shown her all she could have, with a ready-made family and shared traditions. Brady, as usual, was adorable. He'd spent every minute with her talking about how much his dad liked her and how much fun they'd all have together. She'd left her bubbe's apartment filled with dreams of the future. And back at Shane's house, their chemistry had been off the charts.

As she lay sleepless in bed, she couldn't help the rush of emotions that filled her—love and desire washing over her.

And even this morning, when Shane had shown up at her office with flowers, flowers that had her name as part of them, she'd gone all starry-eyed at his thoughtfulness. She'd been useless at work, creating image plans for clients designed to fulfill all their dreams, rather than practical advice they could follow and see measurable results.

But it wasn't until she'd returned to Bubbe's apartment that her world fell apart.

"Hi, Bubbe!" she'd called out to her grandmother as she entered the apartment. "I've brought groceries. This is the last of the Passover stuff on your list."

"Thank you, sweetheart. Just set it there."

Naomi placed the bag on the granite countertop and

began unloading. She smiled as she saw the baked goods from yesterday in packages on the counter.

"Yesterday was so much fun," she said. "I hope it wasn't too much for you."

"Pfft, I'm not that old, Naomi."

"I know you're not, but you're also not used to an energetic six-year-old."

"Brady was very well-behaved and a joy to have around." She gave Naomi one of her piercing stares. "You seemed to enjoy Shane's company."

Naomi's chest swelled. "I did. That man…" She couldn't possibly confess what they did after baking the Passover treats, but as her cheeks heated, she suspected her grandmother had some idea.

When the older woman didn't smile back, Naomi paused. "What's wrong, Bubbe? Didn't you like Shane?"

"I liked him very much. He's handsome, polite and has a good head on his shoulders."

"Then what aren't you telling me?"

"Did he mention my conversation with him?"

Naomi nodded. "He said you two talked about religion and future plans for a family. Bubbe, don't you think that was a little out of line? I didn't ask you to talk to him about any relationship we might have."

"I know you didn't. But the last thing I want is for you to be hurt again."

"I don't want that, either, Bubbe. But we're not there yet. We're taking things slow. I brought them along because baking is a fun family activity that we could include Brady in. Not because I was trying to do anything religious. And as for any future plans…that's up to me to decide when and how we confront it."

"But that's just it, *bubbelah*. You can't put off the conversation any longer. Not when the two of you are clearly falling for each other. When two people come from different religious backgrounds, they have to have the discussion early, especially when there are children involved. And speaking of children…" Bubbe pinned her with a look that was both sympathetic and sharp.

Naomi's chest tightened.

"Have you talked to him about whether he wants more children? Or his feelings about adoption? Have you told him what happened with Andrew?"

A chill washed over Naomi. Not in so many words. They hadn't really discussed children since their original date all those years ago. And despite his conversation then about adoption, seven years had passed. And he'd chosen someone else.

"I told you the other day I was going to talk to him."

"If you wait until you can't live without the other person before discussing such important issues, what will you do if it turns out he has a completely opposing view than you?"

"I'm not thinking of waiting until we get married—not that we're getting married in the first place," she said, despite what her heart had told her last night, "but we literally just started seeing each other. I think we have a little time to figure out exactly how to broach the subject."

"Do you trust him?"

That was the million-dollar question. She did. Or at least, she thought she did. Then why was she so afraid to ask him if he'd be willing to adopt?

Reaching for her grandmother's hand, Naomi squeezed. "He's a good man, Bubbe."

"He is. But the two of you together is complicated. I'm not suggesting that you and Shane are a bad thing. I'm well aware I'm the one who commented on how great he was in the first place. I just think you both really have to go into a relationship with eyes wide-open."

Eyes wide-open.

That was what made Naomi pause. Because that meant letting down all her walls. Letting him in completely, and trusting that he wouldn't turn around and hurt her. Or change his mind. He was kind and considerate, but his first responsibility, as it should be, was to Brady. What if he decided a relationship with her wasn't what was best for Brady?

Her fears were only one part of her new reluctance. The other was the strength and speed of her feelings. She hadn't expected to fall so far and so fast for both him and his son. She hadn't expected to need Shane as much as she needed air to breathe. She'd finally accepted herself after Andrew dumped her. What if Shane decided that their differences were too much to overcome? She'd fought too hard to accept her own worth, to being on her own, to turn around and rely on a man—a wonderful man—for her happiness.

No, she needed to slow things down, take a step back, and think.

Her heart ached at her need for him, and the thought of going without him. If she really cared for him, though, she'd make sure they were both ready for what came next.

Closing her eyes, she picked up her phone. She had to call to cancel tonight. She opened her eyes and dialed his number.

The sound of his voice made her tremble. His excitement at speaking to her, and at seeing her later, should have thrilled her. Instead, her eyes filled with tears.

Could he tell from her tone what she wasn't saying?

"I can't get together tonight after all," she said. It was the truth, but it only gave part of the story.

His concern tore at her. How had she ever thought he was superficial or using her until someone better came along? It took all her concentration not to burst into tears.

Canceling their plans cut her to the core. Because, deep down, she didn't want to spend the evening without him. After last night, being alone was never going to be the same.

She gave a noncommittal response when he asked about seeing her tomorrow and hung up the phone. Then she climbed into bed and cried.

For the next week, worry constantly ate at Shane. Naomi was avoiding him. What if he'd done something to make her change her mind? After she canceled their date night, he'd followed up the next day, but his call went to voicemail. He stopped by her office, but she wasn't there.

His nerves increased. He didn't want to fall back into his old ways of assuming he'd done something wrong, but what other options were there? She hadn't sounded right on the phone. Maybe she was sick. She lived alone. Perhaps she needed help. He went to her apartment but no one answered his knock. Now he was really concerned. He texted her, his last resort before he went to her grandmother's apartment to see if the older woman knew where Naomi was.

Finally, Naomi answered, but her text confused him even more.

I think we need some time apart.

He'd stared at the message, words blurring in front of him.

What did she mean? Was his original fear, that she'd changed her mind, right?

He tried calling her, but she didn't answer, so he was forced to have the conversation via text.

What does that mean?

We're moving too fast and I'm not ready.

I can go slower.

Please, just give me some space.

She'd been so warm and involved, and suddenly she wanted space? How could one person change so suddenly? Or had it been him all along? He'd never been the kind of guy to force himself on someone, so he listened. He gave her what she wanted. But the week apart was one of the worst he'd ever experienced. The only thing worse was his divorce, but at least he'd had the pleasure of Brady.

This time around, his son was old enough to notice Naomi's absence and comment on it.

"What did you do, Dad?"

Great, just great. "I don't know, Brady. Sometimes adults just don't work without knowing why." But it was a stupid answer. He needed to know just as badly as his son.

"Well, that's dumb. Naomi's great, and I want her as my stepmom. You need to fix this." He glared at his dad.

If only it were that simple.

But maybe that was also part of the problem.

Although she hadn't said much during their time together, Naomi's text had complained at how fast things were moving. If he took a step back and analyzed things from her point of view, he had to admit she was right. From the moment he'd walked into her office, all he'd talked about was finding a stepmom for his son. He hadn't given a whole lot of attention to just getting to know each other and enjoying each other's company.

It was one thing for his six-year-old son to move the players on the board three steps ahead. It was another thing entirely for the adults to jump ahead twelve.

If only she'd talk to him, he could find out if that was the problem. But after that one set of texts, she'd gone radio silent, leaving him alone with his thoughts. He spent the time trying to work, but after asking Raul to repeat his reports multiple times, he called his family and told them he was taking a few days off.

That must have set off a family alarm because Micah and Poppy hunted him down that night. They showed up at his door with alcohol and food.

"Hey," he said, opening the door. He frowned, stress making him bone tired. All he wanted to do was go to bed.

For a year.

They looked him up and down, and he wished he'd pretended not to be home.

Micah shoved past him. Poppy gave him an apologetic look, but followed her cousin inside.

Well, Shane wasn't about to leave his own home, especially not with these two here. Micah would look around in distaste and probably hire his decorator to redo it, and his sister would undoubtedly try to help, too, turning his home into the mini version of his parents' home, just like Poppy's was. His already sour mood fell further.

"What are you doing here?" he asked when he reached the kitchen.

Poppy was opening his cabinets and pulling out plates. "Feeding you."

Micah rummaged in his drawers, finding a bottle opener. "Watering you." He looked at his cousin and grinned.

"I'm not a plant. And I don't recall inviting you, although I won't kick you out. Yet."

When she'd finished putting out the food on the kitchen island, she stacked plates, utensils and silverware, spreading her arms at her display.

"You're unhappy," she said.

"Yeah, your brain has been somewhere else," Micah added.

Shane scowled as he took one of the proffered beers. "And you think alcohol is going to help?"

Micah pounded him a little too hard on the back, and Shane had to grip the bottle tight to avoid spilling it. "You're not a rocket scientist or in charge of the nuclear codes. Therefore, alcohol won't do any immediate harm and might encourage you to let off a little steam."

"Or at least tell us what's wrong so we can help," Poppy said.

"Houston Black and Mockingbird acted up when you were around, so if only for the horses' sakes, you need to snap out of whatever's bothering you," Micah insisted.

"Your empathy is astounding," Shane said to his cousin. But if even the animals sensed his troubles, he really did need to do something. He sighed.

"Should we let him eat first?" Micah asked Poppy, as if Shane wasn't sitting with them.

"We could, although—"

"I'm right here," Shane said. "Jeez, you guys are pains in the butt, you know that?"

Poppy grinned. "That's why you love us."

He reminded himself just how much he did love them instead of giving them some flippant remark he'd regret later.

Giving in because he realized these two weren't about to back down, he served himself the chili and corn bread Micah and Poppy had brought, grabbed another beer and sat at the table. His cousin and sister followed him. Slowly, as he ate, he described what happened between him and Naomi.

"Of course she needs space," Poppy said when Shane had finished. "You're super focused and go one hundred miles an hour toward whatever your goal is. But not everyone can keep up with you. Naomi needs time to process everything and make sure that what the two of you want can mesh."

Micah nodded. "I agree. But that doesn't mean you have to go no contact."

"I'm not the one who isn't responding," Shane grumbled.

"Send her flowers. Or a love note. Leave her a voicemail just telling her you're thinking of her."

"Just don't go all stalkerish," Poppy added.

"I'm not an idiot," he protested.

"Never said you were, but I did say you're super focused," she said.

He grunted. They weren't wrong.

"How long do I need to give her space?"

"When was the last time you contacted her?" Micah asked.

"A week ago."

Poppy nodded. "You could do one of our suggestions. Let her set the pace though. If she doesn't respond, don't force it. And if she does, be gentle."

Gentle. He could do that.

When the three of them finished eating, Micah and Poppy cleaned up, gave him a hug and left. The house was empty once again. Too empty. But maybe if he took their advice, he could get Naomi to talk to him.

He'd start with a voicemail. If she needed space, low-key was the way to go, and that was the most low-key of all the suggestions.

He dialed the phone, intending to leave a brief message saying he missed her and hoped she was doing okay.

But she surprised him by answering. His words, his thoughts, fled.

"Hi." Her voice was soft and sad.

"I didn't expect you to answer."

"I wasn't going to."

He swallowed, trying not to be hurt. "I was planning to leave you a message."

"You can tell me now if you want."

He blew out a breath. "I just wanted to check in with you, ask how you were doing and let you know I miss you."

Silence greeted him. But this time, instead of beating himself up about what he might do differently, he waited. She wanted space. That applied to all things, including silence on the phone. He sank onto the sofa and waited her out.

Finally, his patience paid off.

"I miss you, too," she said.

He didn't want to be happy about her comment. It meant she was in as much pain as he was. But he couldn't help the relief that coursed through him. It meant he still had a chance. Repeating the word *space* in his head, he rose from the sofa and paced as he spoke. "Is there anything I can do to help you? It's okay if there isn't. I just hate that you sound so sad."

"I'm scared. And overwhelmed. And I don't know how to navigate a way forward."

She was scared? Of *him*?

"Maybe I can help," he said. "I'm trying to understand

how you're feeling and what it means for us, but I'm confused. Probably because we haven't talked for a while. I really want to help. I don't know what I can do about it, but without knowing anything, it all falls on you. Maybe there's a way to navigate this together."

She laughed without any mirth. "I'm supposed to be the image consultant, so how come you're the one making all the sense?"

"I had a great teacher."

She paused a beat before continuing. "Our passion is so strong, our relationship is moving so fast, that I feel unmoored."

"I'm sorry," he said gruffly. His sister was right. He'd gone too far too fast.

"I have such strong feelings for you, they scare me. With Andrew... We were together for long enough that I thought we were on the same page. Obviously, I was wrong. So with you, and how fast we've moved... I'm afraid I'm making the same mistake twice."

He couldn't help the pride that made his chest expand. "If it helps, I've never felt this way about anyone, either. And I don't foresee that changing in the future."

"Why is it happening so fast?"

He had no idea. "Maybe it's one of those things that people say, when it's right, it's right."

"Or maybe it's all physical attraction and it's going to burn out just as fast. Especially because of our differences."

Hope plummeted. "Do you think that's it? Because I know we're different, but that's one of the things that draws me to you."

"I'm so scared to move forward and get hurt, or to hurt Brady."

He blew out a long, slow breath. "Naomi, I know I said

in the beginning that chemistry was important. And it is. But what I feel for you is so much more than chemistry. I care about you, inside—your hopes and your dreams. I want to share in your joys and your sorrows. I want you part of my existing family." He swallowed hard. "And I want to build a family with you, as well. It's why Brady's opinion of you is so important to me. I want to be part of your life— your traditions, everything. Yes, it's fast, and yes, it scares me, too. But honestly, being without you scares me more."

Her silence made him wonder. Was she pacing, like he was, trying to work out how their relationship could thrive? Or maybe she was sitting, biting a nonexistent cuticle on her perfectly manicured nails. No, he couldn't picture that. Naomi was too polished. Maybe she was chewing her bottom lip, the pillow-soft one he'd kissed, wondering if what he said was true.

Just as likely, for all he knew, she was trying to figure out a way to let him down gently.

He ran a hand through his hair, wishing they were talking in person. If he'd known they were going to have this conversation right now, he would have gone to her to plead his case in front of her. But he'd assumed he was leaving her a voicemail.

Just as he was about to suggest they get together to hash it all out, where he could see her beautiful face in front of him, she cleared her throat.

"Being without you scares me, too."

He shouldn't revel in her fear, except it meant she cared. Fear was holding her back. Growing up on a ranch, he knew how to deal with scared horses. Slow and steady.

He let out the breath he'd been holding.

She spoke again, before he had a chance to respond. "What about children? And Brady? What if we don't work?

Or what if blending different religions, or adding siblings, confuses him?"

She wanted children with him. Elation rushed through him. But still, he paused so as not to overpower her. "I've put Brady first his whole life, and I'm going to continue to do that," Shane said. "I don't want anything we do to hurt him. But I don't think adopting children or sharing different religious traditions is going to hurt him. His mother and I got divorced and Brady survived. We've worked hard to give him two loving, stable environments, and we've made sure he knows he's always our priority."

It was the one thing he was most proud of.

"I hope, more than anything," he continued, "that you and I succeed. But God forbid, if we don't, I'm confident that Brady can get through it, because I'd never fall for someone who wouldn't do her best to shield him from as much hurt as possible."

He'd pled his case. He didn't know what else to do. Maybe he really should go over there. He rose, holding his phone to his ear, grabbed his keys and raced out of the house. It took every ounce of strength he had not to slam into the body that stood on his front porch. Only by dropping his phone and reaching out blindly for anything to stop him did he manage to avoid knocking Naomi down. Instead, he slammed into the porch railing.

The jolt knocked the wind out of him, and it took him a few seconds to recover.

It took him less than that to realize she was here, calling his name.

"Shane! Shane! Talk to me."

He nodded, unable to speak from a combination of oxygen loss and overwhelming relief that she was here. On his porch.

"I'm fine." He pushed the words through, pulled her to him, and squeezed her tight. "Now that you're here."

All thoughts of going slowly, giving her space, slow and steady, evaporated. He couldn't let her go. Not now that he had her in his arms. He breathed in her light floral scent, felt her heart beat against his chest. Closing his eyes, he clung to her, running his hand through her hair.

A squeak made him realize how tight his hold was, and he loosened his grip only slightly.

Okay, maybe I shouldn't abandon all thoughts of slow and steady.

"Thank you," she said, a wry smile on her face. "Death by Shane is probably the best way to go, but still, I'd like time to enjoy you." Her gaze turned serious. "And we still have a lot to talk about."

Time. She needed time.

"I know," he said. "I was on my way to you."

He led her into the house, not letting go of her hand, but this time allowing her to breathe. Once inside, he sat with her on the sofa.

"The first thing I want to say is I love you, Naomi Katz. I should have said it earlier in our conversation, but I was afraid you'd hang up. I love you. No matter what else happens, even if you decide we aren't worth it—" he swallowed, silently berating himself for offering that as a possibility "—I want you to know that."

She closed her eyes and a tear escaped, trailing down her cheek.

His chest seized.

"I love you, too," she said. "I think I have since our first pretend date, when you spilled water on me."

He laughed, more of a way to release tension than anything else, and they exchanged a glance, the kind that long-time couples with a private joke shared. He waited.

"But that's not going to help with the things we have to talk about," she continued.

Maybe she didn't think so, but as long as he knew they loved each other, he was positive they could work out the rest. He let go of her hand, but stayed nearby.

"You come from a big family, and I've always wanted that, but the only way that will happen for me is through adoption. It's taken me a long time to accept that I'm a full person even if I can't give birth, and I'm not willing to lose that."

She was thinking about kids. With him. Hallelujah.

He held up a hand to stop her. "I'd never think you were less than perfect, even without being able to have children of your own. Whether we adopt one or ten or something in between, your worth will never suffer because of me."

Her shoulders relaxed. "Your family has its own traditions," she said. "And I want to learn about them. I'd never ask you to give them up, but you've seen how important my religion is important to me. It's fraught with all kinds of complications, but despite all of that, or maybe because of it, if we were to someday have kids, I'd want to teach them to follow my religion, too."

"And I want to learn right along with them," he said. "Heck, I'm happy to start learning now. My family's traditions are important to me, of course, but mostly because of the chance they offer us to get together. I'd want us to celebrate Easter with my family, because it's an opportunity for everyone to be together. I've never been a particularly observant person, and I'm more than willing to support you and any children we might have as you embrace your religion. And be an ally when you need it."

Her eyes flickered with hope and something else. "When we first had our date seven years ago, you were the first person to remind me that I could adopt, that there was more than one way to have children. But then you left as soon as Lacey showed up, and I felt like I was tossed aside."

Shane's throat thickened and he reached for her. "I'm sorry. You'll never know how much I regret how I treated you."

She held up a hand. "I know. And then I met Andrew, and I thought he was okay with my inability to have kids." She glanced sideways. "Until he cheated on me, telling me he wanted biological kids of his own."

Rage sliced through Shane's chest. "Anyone who would cheat on their partner is horrible."

Her smile flashed for a second.

"You know I'd never do that, right?" Shane asked.

She nodded. "But what happens if you decide you want more biological children? I can't give them to you, and I've finally reached a place of acceptance. I don't want to deprive you of something you might want, but I also don't want to be hurt if you change your mind."

His heart tugged with sympathy. "I'm not the same guy I was back then, Naomi. I can't predict what I'll want or not want at some distant time in the future, but I can promise you this. I know what you bring to this relationship, and if I had any doubts, I'd never have let it get this far."

She twined her fingers through his and squeezed. The pressure loosened the tightness in his throat, and for the first time in what felt like forever, he relaxed.

"It's not going to be easy," she warned, looking at him from beneath her lowered lids. Her focus was still on their hands, but he took heart from that. When she stared into space, she tended to see hurdles that he didn't know how to cross alone.

"Nothing worth it ever is," he said, reaching for her chin and turning her toward him. "And in case you have any doubt, let me make myself perfectly clear. You. Are. Worth. It."

Letting go of his hand, she wrapped her arms around him, drew him close and kissed him. Her soft lips joined with his in the sweetest way he'd ever experienced. A rush of tenderness flooded him as he conveyed his love without words. When they finally broke apart, her eyes sparkled with unshed tears, his pulse pounded in his ears and nothing mattered but making this woman happy.

"You're worth it, too," she whispered.

Over the next week, Naomi talked with Shane every day. Some days it was in person, something she liked the best. She loved being in his presence. His size, his scent, his ability to make everyone around him feel special—she treasured it. She loved how when they talked, he focused on her words. Oh, she knew he was attracted to her. Their chemistry was incredible. It was like the pheromones had a dance party every time she and Shane were within feet of each other. But he made it a point to show her how serious he took her concerns. They talked about religious differences, how to handle those differences with each other and with Brady, antisemitism, holidays, food. They discussed her dreams about adopting children, and his eagerness to do so. They talked about her job and his. And he showed her in all kinds of ways how trustworthy he was. Little things like calling her when he said he would, or following up with something they'd discussed in the past.

Other days, when the two of them had busy work schedules or she had to give her grandmother extra help for Passover, they texted and talked on the phone. Those conversations tended to be lighter, more of a check-in than anything deep. But she'd begun to crave the sound of his voice, the way he pronounced her name, his tone when he told her he loved her. And little by little, her trust increased.

Her parents had just returned from their trip, and they were all at her grandmother's apartment, putting the finishing touches on Passover preparation.

"Bubbe mentioned you're seeing Shane Fortune," her mother said as she and Naomi polished the silver and ironed the white cloth napkins. Her mom's wedding ring flashed as she moved the iron across the board.

Naomi's cheeks heated. "I am."

"You're happy."

It wasn't a question, and Naomi studied her mom. Energetic and wise, she'd never been able to get anything past the woman as a child. Now, as an adult, she didn't want to, but she did want to be sure she understood her own thoughts.

"I haven't been this happy in… I don't know when," she said. "I'm not even sure I was as happy as I am now while I was dating Andrew."

Her mom's face spread in a grin, her brown eyes softening. "That's wonderful. I'm glad to see you've gotten your joy back. I've missed it."

Naomi relaxed. Now she just needed to get her grandmother to understand.

"You invited him to the seder, right?" Bubbe walked over and held a spoon up to the light. Seemingly satisfied, she replaced it in the "done" pile.

"I haven't yet, Bubbe. I wanted to make sure you were okay with Shane and Brady being included in my life."

Her grandmother's look of surprise turned to shame, and she rushed over and gave Naomi a hug.

"I'm sorry, sweetheart. I never meant you to think I objected to your relationship with Shane and Brady. I had my concerns about your different backgrounds. I still do. But I trust you to make your own decisions about who you love, and if you love him, that's good enough for me."

A weight lifted from Naomi's shoulders. "Thank you." She hugged the older woman back. "We've had more conversations about our backgrounds than almost anything else this past week. We've laid the groundwork for our future, provided the future is one we both want, and we've addressed a lot of areas of potential conflict." She sighed. "And you're right, it's complicated, but we both want our relationship to work, and we're equally interested in each other's traditions. Honestly, I love learning about the things he and his family do to celebrate holidays, and I think there's the potential to do so much good together."

"That's wonderful," Bubbe said.

Her mother agreed. "Now go invite him!"

With a laugh, Naomi put down the silver and reached for her cellphone. She dialed Shane's number. When he picked up, Naomi spoke.

"Would you and Brady like to come to our seder tomorrow night?"

He answered right away. "I'd love to, but are you sure it's okay for a six-year-old?"

Joy washed over her. "Oh my gosh, yes. Seders are meant for kids, too. He'll have lots of fun. There's even a hunt for matzah during the dinner, remember?"

"That's right. I remember how excited Brady got when you told him about that." He cleared his throat. "We'd love to come. What time, and what can we bring?"

"Five o'clock and just yourselves. Seriously, there's special ingredients for everything, so you're better off not bringing anything."

"Okay, we'll see you tomorrow night."

She hung up and turned to her grandmother, her body humming. "They're both joining us."

"Terrific. Now we just need to add two more chairs, and maybe an additional leaf to the dining table. Hmm, I wonder if I have enough food or if I should make more?"

"No!" Naomi and her mom both shouted. "You have so much food, Bubbe, we could invite an entire extra family and still have leftovers."

"If you're sure," she said, a frown marring her features. "Maybe I should just add another dessert…"

Naomi and her mom exchanged looks, knowing no matter what they said, her grandmother would never be convinced. The leftovers would carry them through much of the eight-day holiday.

She couldn't wait until tomorrow.

Chapter Ten

Shane and Brady entered Bubbe's apartment the next evening to the aroma of matzah ball soup, onions, garlic and other flavors he couldn't identify but looked forward to eating. His mouth watered. Raucous chatter filled the apartment, and Brady stuck to his side, overwhelmed by the prospect of meeting so many new people.

Naomi, followed by Bubbe, greeted them at the door.

While Bubbe gave Brady a hug, Naomi kissed Shane, not nearly as long as he would like, but with the promise of more to come later.

She pulled away. "I'm so glad you're here."

"Me, too. Before I forget, will you come to my mom's Easter celebration with us? It's just dinner and an egg hunt."

She nodded. "I'd love to." She turned to Brady. "Are you ready for your first seder?"

He shrugged, and Bubbe patted his head. "Don't worry," she said. "It can be a lot of fun, and everyone here is excited to meet you."

She led the little boy away to make introductions, and with a backward glance at Shane, Brady followed.

"Hey." Shane pulled Naomi into his arms again. "I missed you."

"I missed you, too. Ready to meet the family?"

He leaned his forehead against hers for a moment before nodding. "Let's do it." Wrapping his arm around her shoulders, he walked with her into the living room.

Since the last time he'd been here, the entire place had been transformed. The green-and-blue dining room, right off the living room, boasted a huge maple table, the same one he'd sat at when it was just the four of them, but which now held multiple leaves to accommodate all the guests. At the end of the dining table, another folding table had been added. The blue and silver living room sofa, matching chairs and marble coffee table had been pushed to the perimeter of the room, and folding chairs surrounded both the table and the edges of the room as well. It looked a little crowded, but the smiles and laughs of the people in the room told him people were more concerned with being together than having a matching, pristine room. His muscles relaxed, no longer concerned about Brady destroying anything.

One by one, Naomi introduced him to her family, starting with her parents.

"Mom, Dad, this is Shane. Shane, these are my parents, Lenny and Renée."

The suntanned couple smiled and stuck out their hands. "Naomi's told us a lot about you and your son," Lenny said.

"It's great to meet you," Renée added.

"Great to meet you both," Shane said. "How was your trip?"

"Just wonderful," her mom said. The four of them chatted about their vacation, until Naomi pulled Shane away to meet the rest of the relatives.

"This is my aunt Debbie and uncle Noah," she murmured. "They're my mom's sister and brother-in-law."

"Nice to meet you," Noah said. "Brady is your son?"

Shane nodded.

"He's adorable," Debbie said.

They chatted for a couple of minutes, until Naomi introduced him to her mom's other siblings.

"Uncle Mark and Aunt Ann, this is Shane."

"A pleasure," Ann said. "You're a Fortune, right? We love your spa."

"My sister runs it," he said. "I'll be sure to tell her."

The cousins, who ranged in age from ten to thirty, waved hello. The younger ones entertained Brady, putting him at ease. Shane breathed a sigh of relief that his son was so welcomed into the family.

"Okay, everyone, let's get started," Bubbe said. "The kippahs are over here for those who wish to cover their heads."

Shane glanced at Naomi. "Men cover their heads with a skullcap during religious ceremonies," she explained. "We're in a home, rather than a synagogue, so it's entirely up to you whether or not you want to wear one. No one will be offended if you don't."

Shane looked around. Since all the men were taking one from the pile, he did, too. After watching how they fastened it at the top of their heads with a clip, he did the same, and then took a seat. Brady sat in between him and Naomi.

Like they were a family.

In front of him, and everyone else, was a book.

Naomi leaned over. "That's called a Haggadah. It's basically a program for the seder. It tells us what to do, what prayers to say, and tells us the Passover story."

Bubbe recited the blessings and lit the candles and then everyone passed around bottles of wine.

Shane poured wine for him and for Naomi. She, meanwhile, poured Brady some grape juice.

Copying what everyone else was doing, Shane raised his

glass as Noah recited the prayer over the wine. He sipped the red wine. It was dry, like he preferred.

Brady smiled with his purple lips. "I love grape juice."

Mark spoke to the group. "Anyone who'd like to do the handwashing, now is the time. As the rabbi said, we wash our hands prior to the ritual of dipping, which we'll do later, to ensure our food remains pure."

"Can I wash my hands, Dad?"

Shane looked at his son. "Never in the history of parenthood has any parent ever said no to a child who requested to wash his hands."

Naomi laughed and brought him over to the bowl. Shane watched the two of them as they washed their hands, pouring the water over each other's hands carefully and then drying them.

He wasn't completely sure he understood everything that was going on, but he was positive that any religious ritual requiring hand washing was a good thing.

The seder continued with parsley dipped in saltwater to represent the tears of the Hebrew slaves.

Shane tasted his. It tasted…like salty parsley. He looked at Brady, who was licking the leaves. Leaning forward, he started to say something, but Naomi caught his eye.

She shook her head, and Mark held up three pieces of matzah.

"The matzah reminds us that there was no time to let the bread rise when the Hebrews were escaping from Egypt. Instead, they had to take with them what they had because they were in such a hurry."

Mark took the middle piece of matzah and broke it in two and put the larger part in a silk bag. "This is called the *afikomen*." He smiled. "Brady, at some point during the meal, this *afikomen* will be hidden somewhere in the apartment. After dinner, you're going to have to find it."

"Wait, don't we get to help?" one of the cousins asked. The rest of them, even Naomi, chimed in.

"Of course you do."

Brady turned to Shane. "It's like an Easter egg hunt."

Everyone laughed and nodded.

"Kind of," Lenny said. "But first, we have to tell the story. Everyone ready?"

Bubbe spoke. "Usually, we have the youngest child at the table recite the four questions." She looked questioningly at Shane. "Would you and Brady like to read the questions in English?"

Shane checked with Brady, who seemed eager, so he nodded. The two of them asked why this night was different from all other nights, and Mark explained. Then, the youngest cousin sang in Hebrew. Brady's eyes widened in awe.

"All right, who wants to play the roles of the four children?" Mark asked.

The cousins, including Naomi, raised their hands.

"I want to be the wicked one," Naomi said.

"I'll be wise," Ben said.

"Simple!" Tamar called.

"Oh, fine, I'll be the uncertain one," Emily said.

As he listened to the four cousins recite their parts, Shane was fascinated by how the Passover story took into account different people's learning styles when teaching about Passover.

Everyone seated around the table read the story of Moses and then it was time for the second cup of wine.

Next, Ann passed around the tray filled with matzah. Everyone said a blessing. Then they passed around a container of horseradish.

"Brady, this one you might not like, and it's totally okay. We eat a small amount of bitter horseradish to remember the bitterness of slavery in Egypt."

Shane decided to try it, and his eyes watered. Brady took a sniff and passed.

"That's probably a good idea," Naomi said. "However, I think you're going to really like this next part," she whispered to his son.

Renée handed a bowl to Shane. "It's apples, cinnamon, a little wine, almonds and sugar," she said.

"It's called *charoset,* and it represents the mortar used to hold the bricks in place when the Hebrews were forced to build the pyramids," Ann said.

Shane spooned some on his son's plate as well as his own.

"Here, put some on your matzah and eat it like this," Naomi suggested.

They copied her, and Brady's eyes lit up. "It tastes like apple pie!"

"And now we make a Hillel sandwich, to combine the bitter and the sweet."

Shane followed everyone's lead, putting some apples and horseradish on his matzah. This was definitely easier to eat, though still not terribly tasty.

Bubbe stood up. As if a signal, four of the others around the table rose and began clearing the table of any unnecessary items.

"Soup will be out in two minutes," she said. Conversations around the table began again.

"Have you ever had matzah ball soup?" Naomi asked Brady, who shook his head no. "You are in for a treat. It's one of my favorite things."

Shane agreed. "It's really good," he said. He met Naomi's gaze. "I've had it at restaurants in Dallas."

The soup was served and conversations quieted as everyone sipped and sighed at the delicious flavors.

"Bubbe, you've outdone yourself again," Ann raved.

"Naomi was an excellent helper," she said. "But thank you."

Naomi laughed. "I'm glad you rescued the matzah balls."

Shane marveled at the flavor. "I've never had soup this good," he said, "or matzah balls this fluffy."

"I use a secret ingredient," Bubbe said, winking. "I'm glad you're enjoying it."

"It's yummy!" Brady cried, making everyone laugh.

Uncle David and his two sons rose when they finished their soup. "Homemade hummus and spinach *keftes* coming up," he cried.

Naomi leaned over. "My uncle makes the best fried spinach patties ever," she said.

While one of the guests collected the emptied soup bowls, another served each person a plate with two *keftes* and a dollop of hummus.

Shane laughed to himself. Naomi had told him the word *seder* meant order. Looking around at the well-oiled machine the family had created in serving and clearing, it seemed to him they'd taken that "order" seriously.

He tasted the hummus and *keftes*. An explosion of savory goodness filled his mouth, and he encouraged Brady to give his food a try.

"Gosh darn it, this is amazing," he said. He searched the table for Naomi's uncle. "Sir, you have outdone yourself." He turned back to Naomi. "Do you have this every seder?"

"We have our traditional favorites, and this appetizer is one of them. But people like to change things up a bit, so sometimes the selection will vary slightly."

"Obviously, I've missed out on lots of good food," he

said, scraping his plate clean. "Do you think they'll let me help clean up?" he asked, nodding toward the people in the kitchen.

Naomi placed a hand on his thigh. His muscle tensed as the warmth from her hand flowed through the fabric of his jeans. For a moment, he wished he could keep it there. He'd missed her touch, even though it hadn't been long since she was in his arms.

"You're the guest this time," she said, "so sit. Later, you can help."

There was going to be a later. He wanted to crow with joy.

Once again, Naomi's relatives rose from the table to clear away the appetizers and help in the kitchen. Shane marveled at how everyone seemed to know when it was time for them to do their specific task. It was as well-choreographed as a line dance, without the music to follow. He compared it to family holiday dinners at his parents' house. As much as everyone pitched in, it tended to be the same group of people who helped. So far, Shane watched various cousins, aunts or uncles bringing out heaping plates of chicken, beef and vegetables, with no one group of people taking over more than others. He'd have to ask how they did it later.

In the meantime, he watched eagerly as platters filled the tables. Aromas—some familiar, some not—wafted free with each dish and made his mouth water.

Naomi took charge of the braised beef brisket, serving portions to each plate passed her way.

Bubbe grabbed pieces of rosemary chicken and potatoes with tongs and added them to each plate. Ann served a rice dish and Renée served something that looked like a potato casserole. Bowls of vegetables were passed around. By the time Shane's plate returned to him, it was loaded with more food than he thought possible. Even Brady's was piled high, and his son looked at him with wide eyes.

"Dad, what is all this?"

Naomi reassured him with a hug around his shoulders. "You have a taster's plate," she said. "We gave you some of everything. Eat what you like, ignore what you don't. Okay?"

He nodded, and once again, Shane marveled how well she handled him.

Brady began to try small pieces of everything. "This is really good," he muttered with his mouth full.

Shane was just glad he liked it. He stopped worrying about manners and dug into his own brisket. His son was right. They were going to have to roll him out of here.

He listened to the talk around the table, subjects ranging from politics to baseball to school sports, and thought about how similar the conversations were around his own family's table. Although, in all honesty, at his family's table, there was a lot of business talk. He guessed that's what happened when your name was Fortune and your family was your business.

If he and Naomi worked out long-term, this kind of get-together was what he had to look forward to. He glanced around the table and caught Bubbe's eye. He tipped his head, and she smiled at him. Was it okay to assume she had gotten past her reservations and was pleased with his dating her granddaughter? Lenny and Renée looked over at him and also smiled. They'd spent a lot of time watching Brady and encouraging him during the seder. Anyone who made his son happy was a good person in his book. He finished the last of the chicken on his plate and wondered if he could take seconds. As if she'd read his mind, Bubbe said from across the table, "Shane, you'll take more, right?"

Well, he wasn't about to offend the woman. "Absolutely."

As if he'd broken the ice, another round of passing the plates occurred. Even Brady asked for seconds of the potato kugel.

Finally, when he was convinced he couldn't eat another bite, Naomi and several of her cousins rose and began clearing the table. He wondered what they'd all do next. His family always turned on a movie after a holiday meal.

But when the dishes were cleared, everyone returned to the table and took out the books again.

Mark leaned forward, eyes gleaming. "All right, kids, are you ready to find the *afikomen*?"

Brady sat up straighter in his seat. "I didn't even see it get hidden," he said, expression filled with wonder.

"That's the point," Bubbe said. "Now, it's hidden somewhere in here," she said, pointing around the room. "Don't go into the bedroom or bathroom, but everywhere else is fair game, including cabinets. And remember, we can't finish the seder until you find it, and if we don't finish the seder, we don't get dessert."

"Whoa, there's *more* food?" Brady exclaimed.

"Yes. And dessert…my favorite part," Naomi told him.

"We know!" everyone responded at the same time, and she laughed.

The adults watched as the kids searched the apartment for the *afikomen*. They lifted up blue-and-silver upholstered sofa cushions, pulled out hardcovers and paperbacks from the bookshelves, and even lifted up the edges of the blue, green and gray plush rugs.

And, surprisingly, no one complained.

He shook his head. After about five minutes, a small voice shouted, "I found it!" One of the girls held up the *afikomen* bag and jumped up and down. Brady was caught up in the excitement, swiveling from the child who found it to Shane.

"You did," Mark said. "May I have it back?"

"No!" all the kids except Brady shouted and began to laugh.

"No?"

They all shook their head.

"Hmm, I wonder what I could possibly give you to get it back…" Mark mused.

Shane laughed at the man fiddling with his chin, as if he were in serious contemplation of a major dilemma. The kids suggested various gifts, and Brady, never having experienced anything like this, just jumped up and down in anticipation along with the others.

Naomi tipped her chin toward the spectacle. "I love this. Makes me wish I was their age again."

"He's not really going to bribe them, is he?"

She nodded. "It's part of the process."

Finally, when excitement reached a fever pitch, Mark rose, feeling his pockets. "I know I have it somewhere," he said.

Then, he reached under the table and pulled out a bag. Stuffing his hand inside, he pulled out small sacks of candy with a little stuffed frog, one for each kid.

Even Brady.

Shane turned to Naomi in amazement. "How did he know?"

"As soon as you and Brady said you'd come for Passover, Bubbe called him and told him to make sure there was enough for him, too."

Shane's throat thickened at their thoughtfulness. Despite the reservations she'd expressed to him, Naomi's grandmother had still gone out of her way to include his son. He looked over at the older woman and mouthed "Thank you."

She smiled.

Once the kids handed over the *afikomen* and had time to try some candy and get over their excitement, Naomi passed out the books again and everyone returned to their seats.

"Time for the third cup of wine and grace after our meal," Mark announced.

Shane listened to everyone recite the blessings, taking a small drink when everyone else did. He looked over at his son, grinning with a purple ring around his mouth. Between the candy and grape juice, Brady's sugar high was at an all-time peak.

Mark reached for a silver goblet in the center of the table. He dispensed wine into the ornately embossed cup, and then Ann poured water into a glass decorated with beautifully colored beads.

"We welcome the prophet Elijah and hope for a better future," he said and recited a blessing. Noah left the table and opened the front door.

"We also recognize the contributions of the midwives in saving Moses and the Hebrew babies, as well as Miriam and the well that offered water to the Hebrews as they wandered in the desert." Ann lifted the cup and recited another blessing.

"Naomi!"

A loud voice from the hallway shouted over the voices at the table.

Brady leaned over. "Is that Elijah?"

Shane looked at the tall man striding over to the table. Naomi's face whitened.

"Naomi, darling." The man rushed around to Naomi. "I made a mistake. I can't live without you. Let's adopt."

"Andrew."

Shane's heart froze. It wasn't Elijah. It was her ex.

The room went silent, except for the rush of blood in Naomi's ears. She didn't know where to look—at Andrew, at Bubbe and the rest of her family, or at Shane and Brady. Her brain processed her surroundings at half speed, and from the heat infusing her, she felt her blood circulating twice as fast as usual to her face.

What was *he* doing here?

"Naomi, I need to talk to you," he said, inserting himself in the space between Shane's and her chairs. The only good part was that his butt wasn't facing her.

Poor Shane. His face was white, his muscles stiff.

"We're in the middle of the seder, Andrew," she said. She was glad her voice didn't shake, even though her body did.

"Please, it's important." He looked around at her family, who alternated their gazes between him and her, as if they were watching a tennis match.

Naomi didn't want to talk to him. She didn't want to see him or be near him. They were causing a scene. But maybe it was better to get him away from Shane and Brady and the rest of her family.

With a nod, she rose.

He pulled her chair out, as if he were a gentleman. She knew better. He only was one when it suited him, when he had an audience. Like now.

"Bubbe, may we use your study?"

Her grandmother's jaw was tight, and Naomi got a surge of satisfaction knowing she was angry. One curt nod was all she gave. Naomi led her ex to the study and shut the door. Thank goodness there wasn't a bed in here. The last impression she wanted to give anyone was that they were going to have sex.

Although the way Andrew walked toward her and placed his hands on her shoulders, he might be under a different impression than she was.

She took a step back.

"I've missed you, Naomi," he said. His voice was cultured and smooth, something she'd once admired.

"What do you want, Andrew?"

"You."

She almost laughed at his brazenness. "You had me, and decided I was damaged goods when you found out I couldn't have children."

He had the grace to look away. "I was…" He ran a hand over his face. "I was misguided."

"Oh really? You just figured that out now?"

His neck reddened. Good, she thought. Let him own what he did.

"Look, I'll admit I was wrong, and it took me entirely too long to figure it out. But we were great together. And we could be again. I'd even be open to adoption if that's what you want. I just know life without you is wrong."

Wrong? She was finally clearheaded enough to really see her ex for who he was. And she didn't like who she saw. He might have been perfect for her at one time, with his polish and degree and his perfect gifts for all occasions. But after just a short time with Shane, she realized what she'd missed.

Shane loved her. He'd welcomed her into his family, he was willing to open himself up to her religion and culture. And she was much more excited about being with Shane than going back to Andrew.

"It's too late. I'm sorry. But I'm not interested in someone who cheats."

He had the grace to look away. "Let me make it up to you. Tell me what to do and I'll do it."

How many times had she wanted to see her ex begging her to take him back? Naomi remembered when he'd first left her, the devastation that penetrated deep in her bones, making her physically ill. She'd looked in the mirror and hated who she'd seen—a body that had betrayed her and prevented her from getting the one thing she, and Andrew, had wanted: a baby of her own. But instead of remaining true to her, Andrew had decided he wanted what she couldn't give him. Now when she looked in the mirror, she loved who she'd become and what she saw. It was a hard-fought win, requiring her to dig deep, but she wasn't about to lose herself.

Not again.

"There's nothing you can do." Her voice was firm and surprisingly unemotional. She looked at the man she thought she'd loved and felt…nothing. It had taken her months to get past him. And, in the short time she'd been with Shane, she'd realized the kind of man she was looking for, and Andrew wasn't it.

"Please, Naomi, give me a second chance. You can't just throw away our years together."

Now she bristled. "I didn't throw away anything. You did."

He looked abashed. "You're right, that was a poor word choice. I'm sorry."

"Don't be. Losing you was the best thing that ever happened to me. I rediscovered myself and who I want to be."

"You can't mean that."

"I do."

She softened. "I'm sorry to be harsh. You'll find someone perfect for you." *Just like I have.*

"You're perfect," he said.

She gave into the smile his comment caused. "I'm not. And I think deep down you know that."

He stared at her in silence, but she didn't back down. After several moments, he exhaled. "Whomever you're with is a lucky bastard." With a flick of his overcoat, he opened the door and strode out of the apartment.

Naomi felt lighter than she had in months. Her shoulders loosened, and the small smile that had started when Andrew told her she was perfect widened into a full-fledged grin.

She left the study and entered the living room, where her family as one turned to her, their gazes filled with sympathy.

Her grin faltered.

The light airy matzah balls she'd eaten only an hour ago hardened into a lump in the pit of her stomach.

Three chairs sat empty at the table.

Shane and Brady were gone.

After a sleepless night where Shane tried and failed to list all the reasons why Naomi would choose him over her ex, he saddled up his favorite horse, Chili Pepper, and went for a ride first thing the next morning. He needed to lose himself in the wind and sun, in the smell of leather and horse, in the sound of hoofbeats. Maybe then he'd be able to think clearly enough to convince himself that Naomi wasn't lost. That despite the mistakes in his past, he deserved the happiness he had with her.

He led Pepper out of the barn, double-checked the saddle girth and swung up onto her back. He hadn't ridden as much, not since Naomi. He'd made a lot of changes since she'd come back into his life. The outer confidence he tried so hard to project was slowly matching the inner one. His muscles protested as Pepper took her first steps, but soon they readjusted to the rhythm of her walk. Shane clicked his tongue, squeezed his calf muscles against her belly and eased her into a gallop. As they crossed the ranch, white prickly poppy blooms passed in a blur, dappling the ground with a green-and-white patchwork.

Did Naomi like poppies? He'd learned a lot of her likes and dislikes over the past few weeks, but he didn't know about poppies.

Gah, he shouldn't think about her flower tastes. He shouldn't think about her, period. Not when her ex-boyfriend was back, ready to be what Naomi needed.

It wasn't fair.

He felt like Brady, crying about fairness. Naomi was more than a toy that got taken away. She was everything. His everything. And just when he'd gotten his hopes up that they could put aside their differences and make their relationship work, her ex returned.

Andrew had shown up, professed his love for her, taken her into a room, and he was left looking like the unwelcome third wheel in a family of two-wheelers.

Her ex was polished and intelligent and successful. He wanted to adopt with Naomi. And he was Jewish.

Shane wasn't unnecessarily hard on himself usually. He knew his strengths and weaknesses. But he couldn't compete with someone who had everything Naomi was looking for *and* had the same religious background as she did. It wasn't right. He wouldn't stand in the way of Naomi getting everything she wanted. So he'd thanked Naomi's bubbe, made his excuses to the rest of the family and, over Brady's objections, left the seder. It was the right thing to do, no matter how dry his throat had been, how hard his heart had pounded against his ribs.

Brady didn't understand, but he was six. He'd learn, or move on, eventually.

But Shane? He wouldn't recover anytime soon.

He'd gotten so close to having it all.

Up ahead, a creek that branched off the Emerald Ridge River—one he'd played in as a child—flowed, and he pointed Pepper in its direction. The soothing burble usually calmed him. But today, all the water did was echo "you lost" as it meandered its way over rocks.

He let Pepper have her head, and they walked along the creek. The thunder of hooves made him look back from where he came. Another rider approached, and Shane could tell by the way he sat on his horse it was his dad. The older man pulled up, and the two of them stared out at the water.

"Raul said you'd taken Chili Pepper for a ride," Garth said. "I took a guess you'd come out this way."

Shane snorted. "Considering how many acres we've got, that was a heck of a guess."

His dad laughed. "Well, worst case, Topaz and I got to go for a ride." He patted the stallion's neck. She whinnied and then lowered her head to chew on the grass. "Want to talk about it?"

What was there to talk about? "Naomi has a choice to make, and I'm getting out of her way."

"You make it sound like a done deal."

"I'm not sure whether or not it is, but she might be better off with him."

His dad looked at him askance, one bushy eyebrow raised. "Didn't realize you were a wallower."

Shane bristled. "I'm *not* wallowing, I'm a realist."

"Oh, how so?"

"She was head over heels in love with the guy. They dated for years. And he's Jewish, just like she is."

"Most of their relationship was long-distance."

Twisting in his saddle, Shane peered at his dad. "How do you know that?"

The man flushed. Other than right before he was about to blow his stack—and Shane was pretty sure this wasn't one of those times—he'd never seen his dad blush before.

"Dad?"

Garth rubbed the back of his neck. "I might have gone to her for advice."

Shane's eyes widened.

"I'm not too old to admit when I need help," his dad added, clearing his throat.

That wasn't what shocked Shane the most. Well, maybe it was, but equally surprising was that Naomi had helped father *and* son.

His father stared off into the distance. "I needed help fixing my image after the paternity test." He ran his hand down his face. "Honestly, I've needed it for longer than that. And she's the best. She gave me great suggestions for improving my standing around town." He met Shane's gaze. "She's the reason I'm mentoring the high school students."

Shane had thought it was a great idea, but totally out of character for his dad. Now he knew why.

"But she also gave me sound advice for improving my relationship with your mother. She's smart, that one."

Like he didn't already know that. She was probably the smartest person he knew.

"You've never been interested in stupid women."

Shane gripped the reins tight, the leather pressing into his palms. No, he was the stupid one in relationships. And all of a sudden, he was thinking that leaving the seder before he'd talked to Naomi was the stupidest thing he'd done yet.

"Naomi is so smart, in fact," Garth continued, "that I don't think she's fixin' to fall again for her ex. If I were you, I'd turn Pepper around and go after her."

He replayed the events of the seder in his head. Andrew had blustered into the apartment, declaring his love for Naomi. But when he recalled her expression, it wasn't one of delight or thankfulness. It was shock. Shouldn't there have been something else there?

She'd gone into the other room with him, but that was to prevent a scene. The two of them obviously had a lot to discuss.

He'd heard the click of the door as it shut, had felt the weight of everyone's stares on him, and had gone cold. His first thought, after wishing Naomi had simply told the man to go to hell, was to get his son out of there. Because no matter what, Shane had to protect him. Which he'd done, but at what cost?

His second thought had been that she deserved better than him. But Shane *was* better than Andrew. And after all the time he'd spent working on himself, he was finally starting to believe it. He'd never been the one to have a problem with adoption. He'd never protested about learning about her traditions.

And he'd never, *ever*, consider cheating on her.

Shane didn't really need his dad to tell him to fight for Naomi. He was ready to do it all on his own. He shook his head in embarrassment.

"No?" Garth raised a brow.

"Oh, I'm going after her," Shane said, wheeling his horse around. "I just can't quite believe I waited this long." He let out a breath, absently scratching Pepper's neck.

He'd dropped her once when he thought Lacey was his dream woman. He wasn't about to drop her again, thinking that Andrew was her dream man. No, sir.

"Dad, it's great to see you, but—"

His dad waved him on. "Get goin', son."

He kicked Pepper's sides and galloped back to the ranch. Practically skidding to a stop, he flung himself out of the saddle and handed the reins to Raul.

"Sorry, but I've got to be somewhere," he said. "It's a matter of life and death."

Raul's eyes widened, and he rushed forward to cool down Pepper.

"Life and death?"

Naomi's voice from the opposite end of the stable stopped him in his tracks. His heart, already racing from the mad dash back to the ranch, skipped against his ribs.

She was here.

Everything he wanted to say stuck in his throat, making it hard to breathe, much less speak. All he could do was nod.

She stepped forward, still backlit from the early-morning sun outside. "Seems a little drastic, don't you think? I mean…" She spread her arms and turned in a slow circle. "Unless there's some life-or-death emergency that you need to handle, in which case, don't let me stop you."

"No." He forced the word out, his voice hoarse. "Not even life or death could make me leave you."

"And yet you left the seder yesterday."

"I…" He exhaled and thrust his hands in his pockets. "I thought it was the right thing to do at the time. The least disruptive. I was an idiot."

She toed the stable floor with her boot, making circles in the dusty hay. "I feel like you're always leaving me."

His heart cracked at the disappointment in her voice. She wouldn't look at him, and that was even worse.

"I thought I was giving you space, doing what was best for you," he said. "And myself."

She paused in her toe circles, before scraping her right toe harder in a straight line. Like she was digging for the truth.

He wasn't lying.

"How could telling me you love me and then leaving possibly be what was best for me?" Finally, she met his gaze. "I spent all night asking myself why you left. I couldn't come up with a good answer, unless it really was best for you to take the easy way out. So I'm here, to hear it from you."

Her words stung, and he recoiled. "I hate that you think the worst of me...and that my actions have justified those thoughts."

"Then prove me wrong," she said.

He wasn't sure if he heard a dare or a plea in her voice. Intent might be everything, but either way, there was space for him. Only a tiny bit, but space nonetheless.

"You were right," he admitted gruffly. "We are very different people. I saw how worried you were about our different religions." He stuffed his hands in his pockets. "I heard how worried Bubbe was."

Naomi frowned. Maybe she didn't know.

"And when we talked about it and came up with ways to respect each of our religions and honor them, I thought that would be enough."

"It was," she said. "That's why I invited you to the seder. For you to see what my holiday means to me, and for you and Brady to be part of it."

"I did. And I honestly thought we could make it work. But then Andrew showed up."

"I didn't know he was going to. I didn't want him there."

"I know. I never thought you did. But he's Jewish, like you. So that huge part of your life fits with his. And when he said he'd be willing to adopt, well, all the hurdles in front of the two of you seemed to be gone. Your life could be exactly what you wanted with him. And it would be a hell of a lot easier for you."

"So you left."

He nodded. "To make it easier for you. I love you, and I didn't want to stand in the way."

"What makes you so sure Andrew is everything I always wanted?"

"I couldn't get past the idea that your being with Andrew would be so much easier for you. And honestly, I wanted to make things easy for you, even if it made things hard for me."

She shook her head. "I'm a big girl, and I can take care of myself."

"I know that."

"And I don't want Andrew. Yes, his being Jewish definitely makes thing easier." She laughed. "My mom always used to say that. But just because it's easier doesn't make it right. His change of heart over adoption wasn't for any reason other than panic."

Shane frowned.

"He hates being alone. He thought the best way to get me back was to say what I needed to hear. But that doesn't mean he feels the way I do. And it doesn't get around the fact that I can't trust him."

She took another step forward. "And if you had waited until our conversation was complete, you would have known that."

Shane hung his head. "I should have. I'm sorry."

Naomi rocked on her heels. "What did you mean before when you said you were doing what was best for yourself?"

He let out a sigh. Those words had slipped out, and he hoped she wouldn't notice them. But since she did...

"I know what it's like to leave someone for someone else." His neck heated. Gosh, he hated confessing this part. "I'm not proud of what I did to you back then. I regret all the hurt I caused you. And seated at that seder table surrounded by your family, with all their gazes turned on me and Brady, listening to the murmurings behind closed doors, for the first time I realized how awful it is to be the one left behind."

He ran a hand over his face. "Maybe that's something I should have learned before. I let fear convince me you'd want to go back to him, and I wanted to leave before you told me, in front of everyone, that you were choosing him."

"Being left behind is horrible," she agreed.

"I'm so sorry for how I treated you back then," he gritted out. "I know we've touched on it, but I just want to reiterate how sorry I am for hurting you."

She squeezed his hand. "I know."

He wouldn't let go of her fingers, keeping them grasped in his. He had to make her see how good they were together. "Naomi, I love you, and I want to spend the rest of our lives together. You are everything to me, and you make me a better person. And that person is someone who wants to put you first always. I may have handled yesterday wrong, but that's only because I wanted you to have everything you've ever wanted. If you'll marry me, I'll do everything in my power to be the man you make me feel like I can be, and to ensure your dreams come true."

She leaned against him, her eyes brimming with tears. "You *are* my dream."

Elation shot through him. "Do you mean that?"

She nodded. "I hate that you left before I could talk to you, but you're the only person who has ever put me first. Andrew was more concerned about getting what he wanted than making me happy. And when I'm with you, I'm so incredibly happy."

He kissed her, their lips brushing softly together. "I will never stop loving you," he promised. "We can adopt as many kids as you want. You're the most amazing mother, and I can't wait for us to have a family, however that looks."

"You, me and Brady are a family," she said. "Even if we don't have any other kids, I'll love being part of our own little unit."

"You don't object to having more, though, do you?" He waggled his eyebrows, making her laugh.

"Never."

He wrapped his arms around her and held her tight. When his heart slowed, he pulled away from her. Visually memorizing every part of her face, he held tight to her hands.

"Will you marry me?"

Her face wreathed in a smile. "Yes, yes, I'll marry you. But only if Brady says yes."

Shane threw his head back and laughed. "I don't imagine that being a problem."

"Then let's go tell him."

He drew her to his side. His heart was filled with joy, and he couldn't wait to spend the rest of his life with her. They left the stable in search of his son, and the rest of their lives.

* * * * *

Harlequin® Reader Service

Enjoyed your book?

Try the perfect subscription for Romance readers and get more great books like this delivered right to your door.

See why over 10+ million readers have tried Harlequin Reader Service.

Start with a Free Welcome Collection with free books and a gift—valued over $20.

Choose any series in print or ebook. See website for details and order today:

TryReaderService.com/subscriptions